Frederick Lightfoot has had five p[...] including *My name is E* (Sandstone Press) and a collection of short stories *Fetish and other stories*. His work has appeared in numerous journals including Stand, Northwords, Oasis and most recently Tears in the Fence. He is a previous winner of the Skrev Press short story competition.

A novelist of national importance.
Egremont Today, reviewing My Name is E

A writer who proves to be just as gifted as an observer of human behaviour as he is a story teller. Congratulations are more than due to Mr Lightfoot.
Joao Henriques, Chapman

Lightfoot succeeds in producing prose that is innovative, striking and compelling. Authors like Lightfoot restore my hope in the future of prose.
Emily Mahen, The Journal

Beautifully constructed and thought provoking.
Steve Spence, Tremblestone

Passion, politics and intrigue reminiscent of Marques.
Dawn Bruin, Evening News

Frederick Lightfoot is an exceptional prose writer.
Ian Robinson, Oasis

Frederick Lightfoot writes with the confidence of a modern European, a true international.
John Murray, author of
The Legend of Liz and Joe, Jazz, etc

THE EXTINCTION OF SNOW

Frederick Lightfoot

SANDSTONEPRESS
HIGHLAND | SCOTLAND

First published in Great Britain
and the USA in 2014 by
Sandstone Press Ltd
PO Box 5725
One High Street
Dingwall
Ross-shire
IV15 9WJ
Scotland.

www.sandstonepress.com

Editor: Moira Forsyth

The publisher acknowledges subsidy from Creative Scotland
towards publication of this volume.

ISBN: 978-1-908737-53-3
ISBNe: 978-1-908737-54-0

Cover design by Mark Blackadder, Edinburgh
Typeset by Iolaire Typesetting, Newtonmore
Printed and bound in Poland

For Denise with love

Chapter One

I am sacred, comfot me.

A simple typing error transforms scared into sacred. A simple typing error means that I shall never know whether he was saying comfort me, lavish on me the boundless pit of your motherly love, or come for me, come and save me in your practical mother way from the mess in which I've found myself.

Was it fear or was it simply laziness that led to such a message? Was he so nervous at that point that his mind and eye were no longer in tune? That is something I should consider. I have made endless pronouncements on the nature and relationship of eye and mind. They haunt me now. Or was it simply the laxity of his generation, a generation that abbreviates and condenses, dispenses with vowels, getting rid of anything superfluous.

I've printed the message, of course. I couldn't trust it to the computer, couldn't believe that such a life changing collection of words would be safe inside a machine. Are they actually inside it or do they exist in some other real-ity, waiting to be drawn down? I betray my predilections rather than my age, the artist, techno-sceptic. I grew up when computers the size of entire rooms, large rooms at that, were displayed on science programmes and the prediction was made that within a lifetime we would all be using them, at work, in the home, wherever mankind did business. I probably scoffed, dismissing such a vision

1

as science fiction and fantasy. How I wish that were true, in my heart condemning the messenger, bringing a stale classicism to the tragedy. I would like to escape such banal educated associations but it's impossible. With hard-copy in my possession I read the message continuously, ritualistically, caught in its barbaric web.

I am sacred, comfot me.

I don't feel I can shed any more light on the words, force them to yield their terrible meaning. I just have to read them, speak them aloud at intervals, memorializing the voice that typed them as if he were whispering them to me, consoling me, living in them for me, my paradoxical, elegiac son. Yes, he would leave such a statement. If it wasn't for the fact of what was to follow I might have assumed it a joke, a piece of enigmatic fun. But that wasn't to be the case.

My son, Joseph, my amazing act of creation, Joseph, my beautiful man, was found dead by the roadside on the outskirts of a small French village. The police said his body had been run over a number of times, certainly three times – three separate collisions – but that it was an accident. There was evidence of alcohol and drugs in his body. The police are quite happy with an account of him falling over in some self-induced stupor and unobserved in the dark being hit by any number of motorists.

The reality they depict isn't true. It can't be true. My son never touched drugs. Besides, if you hit someone it doesn't escape you. I've known that for all of his life and longer, known it for more than his scant twenty-six years and I am no forensic scientist, though they would dismiss my knowledge on the grounds that I am a mother, which is apparently an entirely irrational condition.

Chapter Two

My sister Vivien has appeared as if she were a friend casually calling in for morning coffee. On the door-step she laughed when she saw my expression and told me not to worry, she hadn't come to stay. She has persuaded Graham, her husband, to bring her to the sales, and they have booked into a hotel not far from Tottenham Court Road. She sits with coffee cup poised in her hands like a cup of divination preparing to lecture me, reprimand me, to tell it to me just how it is. The encounter fills me with dread. I freely admit that the estrangement was on my part. I was the one that left, insisted I had to leave, circumstances personal, and came to London and reinvented, reconstructed myself, Louise an artist – well art teacher, let's not hide from any truth – later Louise Tennant, married to John, eleven years my senior, the man who looked after me, always looked after me, until now.

Since Joseph's funeral, since that harsh, interminable day, she has telephoned regularly, her voice large and boisterous on the line, checking up on me, she says, cajoling me, instructing me to get my life back together and move on, certain that an elder sister has such vulgar rights. She performs on the telephone as if we have been friends forever, which is a type of forgiveness, I suppose, though forgiveness is the last thing I want. When she first left college she worked as a student nurse for a while, before settling into management in a department

3

store, and assumes the brief experience of some thirty years ago gives her unique insight into what I'm going through, unique insight into any human drama. In darker moments I think I am a source of entertainment rather than sister love.

"You look dreadful," she says, caressing her mug. She is broad and well made without seeming overweight, dressed in a smart pink suit. I insist that I'm fine. "Are you sleeping?" she asks. I should just admit that I'm simply hung over from almost two bottles of wine. I tell myself that it's almost two bottles, not entirely, as if the distinction holds out some hope for me. "How is John?" she asks. "Have you heard from him?"

"Of course I've heard from him," I say sharply.

She gives a brief, sceptical frown and sips her coffee, her two hands covering the lower part of her face as if she is praying. She has quite a lovely face, round with baby smooth skin and piercing black eyes. She is subtle and managerial in her use of make-up. Soon she will start advising me. She is so used to telling people what to do it spills over into her non-work life. She has not come to be with me but manage me. Maybe I should resent that, but in reality I'm desperately grateful.

"You look a bit of a mess this morning, if you don't mind my saying."

Yes, I probably do mind. I don't need to have it spelt out that the telltale evidence of dissipation is so obvious. I could see it myself in the mirror this morning. I will be fifty next birthday and this morning that was how I looked, a woman about to reach a half century. I don't usually look my age. I still have an air of girlishness, too much so at times. People take it at face value, the small-ness, the quiet, and talk down to it, to me. I still have the

4

vestiges of a narrow, quite gamine, well-structured face, but this morning I was blear-eyed, my hair, which I have coloured a lovely sandy-gold, unruly and my lips were caked with last night's wine, a purple crust. My tongue had the same purple shading. It took an age to scrub them clean, lips and tongue. The back of my tongue remains coated because I couldn't reach it without gagging and retching. My eyes were marked with deep black circles, and spider-lines were apparent across my usually pale-grey skin, the way fine lines form across old porcelain.

"No, I don't mind," I say and smile. "What are sisters for if not brutal truth? I've just had a bit of headache, that's all, well thumping, in fact."

"Have you taken something?"

"Of course, paracetamol first thing, before anything else."

"Well, you need to look after yourself."

"Doesn't everyone."

"You know what I mean."

I'm not actually sure that I do, but it will be a reference to some previous crisis, something I missed because I was in the middle of it, but Vivien will have viewed with interest and stored up for future reference. I reassure her that I'm fine. It is strange talk really, packed with lazy lies and easy concern. Maybe I'm just worn-out with being worn-out and I can't detail it all again, or maybe I suspect that Vivien is less interested than she would want me to believe, and why should she. Mine is a tragic tale, beyond easy reassurance. Why would anyone want to take it on? I should be gentler to Vivien. At least she calls. But I sometimes feel it's to prove to herself that she has no fear. I can imagine her telling Graham how she fearlessly asks for the low-down on dying.

"Are you going back to work?" she asks, with a hint of mild surprise and disappointment in her voice, which I find difficult to comprehend. Does she want me to return, or would it suggest the drama, in which she has positioned herself as a key player, the rescuer, is maybe coming to an end, and that would be disappointing for her.

I shake my head. "No, I'm not going back, not yet. I couldn't face it."

"You should think about it. It's been a while. It might help."

I want to snap at her, demanding to know in what way it might help, in what way exposing myself to design students would compensate for the loss of a child, my child. It's not as if the department has secured my gratitude: one or two visits to begin with and then nothing. Nothing from colleagues I have worked with for years, some openly saying that they couldn't cope. Couldn't cope with what? I'm the grieving mother, the one banished into a place of no life at all. Well, to hell with them. I can't play that game anymore.

"I've discussed it with my counsellor and he thinks it premature."

"You're still seeing him then?" she asks, a certain note of satisfaction entering her voice.

"For a while longer I think."

"Why not?"

Indeed, why not. It takes a certain amount of time and seems to suggest purpose, even if no purpose actually exists. I nod. "The University has been very good," I say, "certainly financially, but I couldn't take on the students at present. Maybe they're too young and I'm too old."

"Nonsense, you look wonderful."

"You said I looked dreadful."

"Usually wonderful, wonderful more often than not. Oh come on, you know you do. You should get out, meet people, see friends."

"Move on."

"Yes, move on."

I half-smile. She is courageous, willing to say it, unlike friends who say nothing. The truth is I don't have friendships anymore I form alliances. Friendships are too difficult. I think most of the friends I ever had have run a million miles. If I'm kind I think it's because they really can't tolerate my suffering, so have excused themselves. When I'm unkind, which is most of the time, I think they're bastards. I need alliances though: the bereavement counsellor, the general practitioner, the support group – Phyllis, Susan, Rebecca, Rami. I am the youngest, by far the youngest, so they mother me, which I appreciate but resent. I want sister care, the way they have it. I don't want to be the exception, the obvious oddity, but I am. They say I am young to be going through this. I find that a strange phrase. Going through suggests an end, a destination. The only end is death. I am not fit for friends, only a courageous elder sibling.

"I don't think I'd be much company for anyone, not yet. People shouldn't have to put up with me."

"You should get out, meet someone. If John won't come home, well hell, why not?"

I can't pretend that I'm not rather shocked by what Vivien has suggested.

"John is working, a lecture tour of American universities. He couldn't turn that down, the opportunity, the prestige, the money. It's what he's worked for. It was too difficult to come home just now, the Christmas break isn't that long. He'll be home for Easter."

7

"He can't cope with you, can't cope with your grieving, so he's done what came natural and run away."

"He has not run away, don't be ridiculous. He's working."

"Who doesn't come home for Christmas, for God's sake, unless there's something to keep them away?" She falls silent, the question poised recklessly, and then she speaks up, boisterous again: "I'm deadly serious, why not? If John sees fit to take off and leave you then what can he expect?"

I should be outraged, defend John, knowing full well that Vivien never has approved, the age difference, the quiet intellectual, the dignity, but of course I've been adulterous before, so I can't exhibit too much shock. There was Frank whom I was seeing when I met John and it was just something that carried on, accidentally, without meaning, certainly without meaning at that stage. With Mushin it was different. He was beautiful, his skin like clay, sun-dried and taut, hot to touch, braiding beneath the palm, his eyes nut-brown, distrustful and alert, yet glad to concede. I'd like to say it was a purely sexual encounter but that wouldn't do it justice. He had witnessed so much, had a maturity that I couldn't comprehend – he claimed that even children in the Lebanon were politically informed – and yet at the same time was childlike and naïve. He was only a matter of years older than Joseph. He would have made a fine artist, but it embarrassed him. He had to be an architect. It was a proper job. He was silly in so many ways. The memory makes me smile and I feel as guilty as hell over that. Did I love him? No, of course not. I only love John.

I can't speak, can't summons the energy needed, but I don't want to break down. It's an old, time-worn attitude

8

of mine. I don't break down with family, elder sister, I remain separate and aloof, but I feel all of my defences crumbling, collapsing under the assault of my brusque efficient senior.

"I miss him," I eventually mutter, "but he'll be home for Easter." I smile, a bluff, hopeless gesture. "I need him around the house."

I can't manage as my own keeper, sole proprietor of a fine house in a home owner's paradise. Today was rubbish day, first day after the Christmas holiday break. I scoured every room for any item of waste. When John is at home it's his job. Naturally, it doesn't do him justice to think of him in conjunction with rubbish sacks, but I can't resist it. He takes care of things; that is what he does, the way things were. He took care of me. I wanted to be taken care of, which makes me sound as if I were a problem or a mission, to which I can't answer. I am running short of answers, but thankfully also running out of questions.

I can smell him in the house, smell him when it's rubbish day. I can smell him as animals are able, aware of presence and absence, but in this case it's not musk and pheromone, the spoor of vigour, vitality and sexual frolic, but gingerbread, newly baked gingerbread. I don't know why. I can logically think of a whole raft of sophisticated foods much nearer the mark, but gingerbread it is, the aroma unmistakable. The thought makes me want to cry. I cry a great deal. I miss my gingerbread man, miss him so much, his scent of calm, his spice. I miss the fact that the business of rubbish is his.

Of course the building is large, many of its rooms no longer in use, one in particular a shrine. Maybe it always was something of an informal shrine, the vacated nest left

9

just as it was, protected by the broody mother. I don't suppose Sara, the other woman, Joseph's wife, mother of my grandchild, would have been too pleased to think that his room had been memorialized. She is a practical, down-to-earth woman, and considered it their room whenever needed, which wasn't often enough. I was always crippled by nostalgia even before I realized it had to exist. I wonder how she feels about events, how her hard-headed, modern woman style copes with disaster. We should speak. We were only polite at the funeral, too overcome I suppose to come together. I should make the first move; I am after all the mature one. If we were members of a pack of baboons or chimps would I not be the alpha female. Though maybe I have it all wrong – yet again, I would have to say – and I was ousted years ago. Maybe it is Sara's move to make, though I know, instinctively, a woman's intuition, that she won't.

I look at Vivien, and can't help but cry. "He hasn't run away from me," I say. "He's run away from himself. He and Joseph had a tough time of it together when John's father was living with us. It was only brief, but it didn't work out. John regrets that, can't cope with it, feels guilty, I suppose." I gaze steadily at Vivien. "I am on my own," I whimper, despite every intention of not doing so.

"You'll always have me," she says, her tone surprisingly brusque, almost stern. If her intention was to stanch any likely outpouring then she has certainly succeeded. "Look," she says, more amiably, "you're right and sometimes a sister has to give some brutal truths, unpalatable truths."

I wait, uncertain and for some reason fearful about what she has to say. I eye her carefully, as a hunted animal might its potential assailant. She forces me to enquire of her what the brutal truth is.

She smiles grimly: "I know that Joseph dying is terrible, I mean, my God, I cannot imagine, really cannot imagine, but I also know you, know what you're doing, taking it all on, wallowing in it, making it about you. It isn't about you, and you need to think about that, think it through and give it up, live again. I know that's what Joseph would want."

"Don't be disgusting," I retort, startled by my own anger.

"I know what you're thinking, about what happened. It was an accident. It was a long time ago and you have to put it out of your mind."

"No," I declare with shocking vehemence. I want to scream it aloud. It was not an accident. There was fault. There was my fault. Instead, I say in a hurt, crushed voice: "Of course it isn't about me, about that. I have his email, his last message, and I know there is something wrong about it, something terribly, terribly wrong."

"There has to be a final email. There's no getting away from that. There's no point dwelling on it, reading things into it that aren't there. Doing that just doesn't help anyone."

I utter it aloud, a quotation, a statement, a fact: "I am sacred, comfot me." Spoken aloud it sounds like, comfort me, but he could have meant come for me. Surely I have failed him. I am sacred, surely it meant, I am scared. The thought is awful. My son was scared, but scared of what. My son was scared and he is now dead. There is something not right. I say it again, wanting to hear the words again, his words, his last utterance to me.

Vivien gazes at me, uncertain, baffled. I can see it in

11

her face, the acknowledgement of strangeness, of things being not right. Eventually she seeks confirmation. "That was the last thing you heard from him? But what does it mean?"

I shake my head.

We sit in silence for a while. Vivien is the first to speak, her voice hesitant, even reluctant: "He rang me a couple of times, before he went away, before he went to France."

"Rang you, about what? He never said that he'd rung you. Why would he ring you?" I ask, uttering the questions quickly, objecting to any suggested intimacy with anyone other than me. I am a jealous mother, not prepared to allow even an aunt admission.

"Joseph often rang, you know that, bridging the gap, the sister gap, the one you make. Joseph liked everyone to get on. He was a party animal, not like you and John. Oh God, don't glare at me like that, you know what I mean. Anyway, he was in Leeds so not so far from us really. Well, a lot closer than when he was in London. He told me he had to do something for John, for his father, but not the things he had been doing. I asked him what he meant but he only said that I'd see, that we'd all see and when we did he'd be pleased, pleased with himself again. He said that with real feeling, pleased with himself again, but when I asked him what he meant he just said he'd been doing stuff he wasn't proud of. He was pretty sure that Sara would never get it, but he had to do it whatever. He said he would be really grateful if I'd keep in contact with Sara, Sara and Georgia. I didn't think anything of it, just that I wasn't so very far away. I said yes, of course, of course I would. We weren't exactly local, opposite sides of the country, but I said I'd do anything that would help."

12

"Help," I repeated, uncertain of the word, of its meaning. "Keep contact as if he knew he wasn't coming back. He knew something was going to happen. Vivien, there is something not right, I know it. I need to find out but I just don't know how."

"Look, don't be melodramatic. It was probably nothing."

"Do something for his father. What? He knew something."

"He could have meant anything, a present, a gift, God, I don't know."

"I am sacred, comfort me. I need to find out. I need to pull myself together. I need to look better than I do."

"I shouldn't have said that. You look great."

"No I don't. I look like hell and I feel like hell, and it has to stop. I have to find out what it means. I have to start somewhere."

"Look, God, don't go off at the deep-end. I know what you've been through and I know how you feel about things, more than you'll ever believe or give me credit for, but you have to keep things in perspective. It's more than likely nothing, the phone call, the email. You know what that generation is like. It was a terrible, terrible accident. A tragic accident. You have to accept that."

"And move on."

"Yes, move on."

I shake my head. But yes, maybe I have moved on. My child's death is not right. I have to deal with that. In some way I have to deal with that.

"There is a piece of music goes over and over in my head," I say, hearing it as I speak. "It's called *Spiegel im Spiegel*, mirror in mirror."

"Meaning?"

13

"I don't know, but something. It's telling me something and I need to see it."

We are silent for some time. Vivien brings it to an end by adopting a managerial, girlfriend attitude. "Anyway, I've brought you a present, a Christmas present for the New Year. New Year, new start."

I've had a present, a Christmas present, and don't understand. I'm obviously something of a cause. I should object to that, but really don't. I look on blankly, saying nothing. "Oh, it's nothing," she says. She hands me an envelope and insists I open it. Inside there is a voucher for a pamper session: massage, hair, nails, Indian head massage, makeover. I thank her. She smiles, evidently pleased with herself. She suggests that we could go together, tomorrow, insists on it, being sisters together, sisters again. Sisters for the first time, I think, but say nothing. I don't feel able to refuse. I commit myself against my better judgement. Vivien leaves with a display of briskness. Today she has to shop, do the sales, but tomorrow we'll meet, a pamper session and then who knows, a meal, a few drinks. She obviously thinks she is making headway with me. Who am I to disabuse her? She is somehow still my sister. She thinks she knows all there is to know. On the other hand, there is so much that I still need to know, it frightens me. Death hangs so heavily on me.

Chapter Three

A day of ice, black, wet pavements, cold enough for a hat and gloves, but no whiteness, no cheerfulness of frost. When I put out the rubbish there were discarded wreaths beside overflowing bins all along Lady Margaret Road – sometimes three or four bins where houses have been turned into flats – the holly still green, the berries shrivelled. Most bins along the street don't have the capacity for an extended break, but some manage, as I have managed. I dread being home all day, the empty rooms, empty time, space in all of its many manifestations. Sometimes I walk up to Parliament Hill, which takes about twenty to twenty-five minutes and go into a café, Paz Bistro, with its welcoming green and yellow awnings and its formidable Italian proprietor who is stern with strangers but to me a charm. Sometimes I pop in and see John's father who is resident in a home there, costs a fortune but John insists on it, when I can stomach the smell of shit, piss and lavender. I know I should go more often. He said to me one day, I like being with us, which I know was beautiful, but I just can't face it.

Today I went to the shops, took a bus to Oxford Street and joined the sales crowds, despite the risk of running into Vivien. I went from department store to department store, enjoying the delicious, cloying must of perfume. It gave me the idea to go in search of blooms, flowers out of season. All I could find were orchids, white-yellow orchids, not cut but in plant-pots. They looked clumsy and deformed, yet somehow beautiful. Despite the inflated price I had to have one, its beauty respite. As I left the shop someone tried to steal a coat, a young girl, but was wrestled to the ground by a security guard, a large, heavy man, who needlessly felt her all over, enjoying himself. I was ashamed to find myself staring at the drama. For a moment, only a moment, I was with the crowd.

I tell my counsellor that I am never lonely, never bored. I have inner resources. I am an artist. I am rich in imagery, correspondence and construction. I am comfortable with myself. It is all lies of course. I crave my men, the two poles of my life. This comfortable home, structured with an artist's eye, is a domestic prison. At least I have the sense to make sure the heating is on, warming the house for my return. In the first months I never thought of it – it is after all an indulgent waste – and used to return to cold rooms. Cold rooms lead to inertia and sterile pleasure.

There wasn't even any solace in eating. In the warmth it's different. There is some comfort. Not that I prepare elaborate meals anymore – not as a general rule, though sometimes I force my hand, make a batch of this or that and freeze it. Old habits aren't so easily broken. My sophisticated manner sticks with me. Tonight it will be cheese and biscuits and wine, more wine than I intend, not because it washes away grief, but rather highlights it, much in the way children highlight the people and things in their pictures with thick black lines. That's what wine does, daubs great thick black lines around things so that they stand out. My mind is a lovely spinning top then, achieving insights and understanding that the bleary morning wipes away completely. Besides, it fills in a bit of space and helps me sleep. If I carry on I'll become a real drunk, lying to myself, living in a parallel world. I should relish the thought. Of course I have more Stilton, Brie and goat's cheese than I can possibly manage, but it was Christmas and habits are habits.

I put out my cheese-board and crackers and lay my plate and glass in the dining room determined to eat in style, with the orchid placed alongside for ornamentation. I consider chancing some music, risk listening again to the music that goes round and round in my head, but before I commit myself the telephone rings. For some reason I don't immediately answer. Eventually I lift it from its cradle and quietly mutter hello.

"It's me," John says, as if responding to my reluctance, the fear of more bad news. There is a period of silence, not necessarily uncomfortable, before John goes on. "How is it there today?"

"Icy cold, but no frost."

"It's cold here too."

"It's nearly Epiphany."

"I know."

"It was bin day today."

"I know."

"They missed out a whole week. Some of the bins are over-flowing. It's all the Christmas and New Year things. There are Christmas wreaths, still green, all right really, except that the berries are a bit shrivelled. You could take the berries off and still have something nice, attractive. I suppose it's over though."

"Yes, I suppose so."

"All over again. Nobody cares about kings bearing gifts. The green Father Christmas used to live until Twelfth-night, but not the red American one. He deposits his presents and then it's all done. Remember we used

17

to eke it out until the bitter end, always sad at the close. Never a lover of God but always a lover of God's things."

"I know."

"You must only have the red one, I suppose, the American one."

"I'm sorry I couldn't make it."

"Vivien says you've run away, run away from me, run away from my grief."

He doesn't immediately answer, and then eventually asks: "Is she there, visiting, staying with you?"

"She was here this morning. She's here for the sales. She wants me to have a pamper session."

"Good."

"Is it?"

"I don't know."

"But you know everything John, that was always the case, everything, absolutely."

"I just couldn't make it. The schedule is too tight. I haven't run away."

"She told me something very strange. She said that Joseph rang her, rang before he went to France. He wanted her to stay in contact with Sara, Sara and Georgia. I don't understand. Tell me John, tell me what to do."

"It was an accident."

"She didn't hold back reminding me about that. That's what you think too, isn't it. The fact that everything is tainted, the fact I can't enjoy anything knowing that someone else never can. You think that's what the problem is."

"I never said that."

"It's no good saying I'm sorry. It doesn't do."

"I never said."

"It was his birthday, you know, a week ago."

"I know Louise, I know it was his birthday."

"Remember how we said it would never have been Holly or Mary if it had been a girl, but we liked Joseph. Maybe we shouldn't have done it. Joseph was a bystander, didn't know what was happening, but our Joseph never was. John there is something not right in all this, and now the phone call to Vivien. I don't get it." My voice lowers, falls, becomes shadow.

John speaks up impatiently, frustrated: "I thought . . . I thought . . ." He gives up, and the sound of his voice trails away.

"You sound like your father when you say that. He said just the same thing one day when he was banging on the walls, I thought, I thought, over and over. It drove Joseph mad."

"I know. I remember."

"I can understand why you were annoyed at Joseph, well, disgusted really."

"That's not true, I just wanted him to appreciate that my father was ill, that it was the dementia that made him do those things. I was never really angry."

"He wasn't intolerant, just scared, scared for you, maybe for himself."

"What do you mean?"

"You know everything, John, you always have, and he didn't want you to ever lose that. He was scared."

"I said he was intolerant. I shouldn't have said that, shouldn't have said a great deal perhaps."

I don't answer. Perhaps John is right and Joseph was intolerant when his grandfather lived with us, but maybe it was understandable. Joseph had always loved his grandfather. When he was young he used to stay with him for a couple of weeks in the summer in a sky-blue wooden

19

house by the sea, and things like that matter. He was such a presence of a man, kind, funny and generous, and now he is only fragments. He was administered a drug for schizophrenia designed to treat his *behavioural and psychological signs and symptoms of dementia*, which the explaining doctor then shortened to BPSD. He curled up at this assault and has never uncurled. He remains hunched still. Joseph simply couldn't bear it. I went to see him on Christmas Day, which at least gave some purpose to my otherwise aimless walk, and the carers played Christmas pop music, put a paper crown on his head, danced in front of him and demanded that he sing up, jollying him along. Why did I let that crown remain? Why was I so powerless? I should have torn it away and trampled it underfoot and insisted that he wasn't a king of fools. Perhaps I am intolerant too.

"Your father looks well," I say, which sounds like the lie it is.

"Thank you for going."

"Don't thank me John, don't do that."

"Louise . . ." John says, but can't complete the thought.

"Why would he ring Vivien?"

"It was an accident."

"No John, I know exactly what an accident feels like. There is something not right."

"Louise . . ."

"What John, what?"

He doesn't reply. I presume he is shaking his head, the runaway husband struggling with my grief, struggling with his grief, working out his guilt.

"You think I should move on?"

"I think we both should."

"Vivien said the same."

"Vivien had a lot to say."

"Vivien always has a lot to say."

"But maybe this time you should listen to her."

I smile. "No, I really shouldn't listen to her, certainly not this time," I say, trying to sound spirited, amused even, but know I sound shrill.

John tells me he has to go. He also tells me that he loves me. He may have run away but he loves me. Do I believe he loves me? Yes he loves me, loves me without reservation, the same way that I love him. Ours was a perfect marriage. Grief has torn it apart. We say goodbye awkwardly, hesitant. He promises to ring tomorrow. He doesn't need to say it. I know he will.

I hear the same message from everyone, move on. My counsellor demands that I accept the reality of my loss, otherwise I won't be able to move on. I don't take issue with him, he is after all an expert, but I have a secret pact with myself. I don't want to move on; I never want to move on. I want to live with my dead for all of my days.

I pour myself a large glass of wine, place the telephone back in its cradle and go from the dining room into the hall. There are beautiful Christmas decorations still on display. I wasn't going to bother this year, indeed thought I probably shouldn't bother, but not to do it, to leave the house undecorated, without a tree, seemed disloyal to Joseph. I told myself that I had to do it for him. I discussed it with my counsellor. He wondered why I should say I felt obliged to do it. He picks up key words and taunts me with them. Obliged, I said, because we always did, it was one of the multitude of things that made us a family, not just people sharing the same facilities – a family of three, I thought, like the holy family, the son

21

destined to die, to die in mysterious circumstances, his memory something to keep alive.

What do you want to do, he countered, underlining the pronoun in his question? If you are saying that you want to decorate the house for Christmas – again emphasising the pronoun – that seems to me a wholly different matter. What could I do but agree with him. Yes, I said, with shyness and a modicum of embarrassment, as if truly caught out, I want to decorate the house for Christmas. And in my mind I added, because I owe it to Joseph. Can a counsellor really be so naïve to think we ever do anything entirely for ourselves, or entirely for others? There is no such freedom on the face of the earth. The germ of every thought was planted somewhere, sometimes in fertile soil, sometimes on scrubland. We are subject to too many cords and binds to be anything but prisoners with privileges. But maybe he knows that well enough, after all he is always trying to get me to talk about my father, something I steadfastly smile away.

Our usual beautiful objects have been packed away, replaced by temporary seasonal ones, but of course all of our Christmas things are beautiful too, painted wood and brass bells, ornaments and candlesticks, nothing ho ho ho, our taste one of a former age. There is a tree in the hallway, not as large as usual but still impressive, decorated with small wooden ornaments, brass pendants, small intricately painted baubles and white lights. We are obviously serious and sober-minded people, if not entirely sober, nothing gimmicky allowed.

Beneath the tree I've put Joseph's letters he left for Father Christmas together with the sketches he did for him. It was a tradition to leave sherry for Father Christmas and a carrot for his reindeer. John would drink the sherry whilst I bit into the carrot, leaving a chewed end. It was Joseph himself, just a child, who started leaving thank you letters and a present of a sketch, usually of Father Christmas himself, a portrait improving year by year. The letter always said thank you for last year's presents, and began by listing them, faithfully recalling the twelve month's previous offerings, but as he got older his memory wasn't quite as good. Either he had more on his mind or got more used to receiving things. We were never averse to spoiling our solitary offspring. I always left a little note in reply, saying what a good boy he'd been and how pleased I was with him and letting him know how much I loved him. I wrote it with my left-hand hoping to disguise my handwriting, maintain the illusion. I was very happy being the left-handed Father Christmas. Joseph was quite happy to let the illusion go on forever. I don't recall that he ever let on that he didn't believe anymore. I wonder if that was for my benefit, a sentimental left-handed Father Christmas, who wasn't a father at all but Mother Christmas, though John was always beside me resplendent in a red dressing-gown.

The first joke Joseph ever got was a Christmas joke. What do you call Father Christmas's wife? Mary Christmas. I remember his face lighting up, and his saying: Oh, I get that one. Of course, Joseph needn't have worried about me. I never did believe in Father Christmas. My sensible, hard-nosed sister Vivien ensured that. On the very first Christmas I ever remember she took me into our parents' room and disclosed the presents hidden beneath the bed, jeering at me for being so stupid. I've never believed in anything, not God, not angels, not Father Christmas, Mary Christmas or ghosts – sadly not ghosts, though I am haunted. We always made a big thing of his birthday, never mixing it with Christmas, one big present or anything like that. He had to feel special. We were that sort of parents.

Have I been a good parent? Was I? I never felt I was. I always seemed to be playing catch-up. No sooner did I feel that I understood something, than it was over and he was doing something else, being someone else, moving away from me and constructing an identity I couldn't influence. I was left high and dry, moonfaced, without a moon's ability to conduct the seas and oceans. The world proved just too big. I remember once when he went on a school trip, all the way to York to see the Vikings, during the five days he was away there was a coach crash involving school children close by and two children died. At the same time two children were caught up in a shooting incident close to a nursery. I remember asking myself how I could ever protect him. The forces ranged against me were so great, too great. I knew even then that I was destined to fail.

Maybe that's why I collected everything he ever did, trying to keep him safe, securing each step of the way. I kept it all, splodges, toddler sketches, nascent shapes, his first interpretation of his world, the budding scientist revealed in every line: collages of witches done in charcoal, calendars, mother's day cards, father's day cards, Easter cards, Christmas cards – the growing skill and accumulation of a life dear to me. I secreted it all away in the loft like an archivist.

Everything is still there, along with all the small gifts he brought into the house, tea-cups from Brighton, models of Leeds castle, soldiers from somewhere or other, and a bust of Shakespeare from Stratford, silly socialised objects too tacky to keep, too precious to dispose of, relegated from shelf to cupboard and then to loft, the lumber of a lifetime's trivial marvels. A lifetime's! It doesn't seem possible. But adulthood was there, waiting with its ceremonies of initiation: the first time drunk, first experience of sex, and whatever new experience this generation invented that mine knew nothing of. For my part there was never any shock, which shocks me now, simply wonder. Where will these irreversible experiences lead the no longer innocent? The fearful world never barked or hollered, never let on about its pack mentality, it just waited licking its lips.

At times it didn't feel as if I was bringing him up but trying to tame him, make him fit into a world over which he had no choice. As parents, or maybe as a mother dragging the father along, we were obsessed by outcome, too obsessed by it. How would it all turn out? The outcome of personality, the outcome of education, the outcome of this, that and the other. We thought as long as he was settled and secure, clean and prosperous, socially conscious, a good person, then we had done well, done our job well. Well, outcome is lying dead on a back road in France. So what was it all fucking well for?

I am sacred, comfot me. What was he saying? How can it all end with that? I should have let him be, not tried to make him anything. The outcome might have been different. It all could have been different. I would so much settle for mediocrity now. I inhabit a house of misconceived purposes.

I put down his notes and sketches, which I've held, I suppose, as if it were his flesh I could hold, and the replies of a left-handed failure, without reading them. I can't do it again. The pleasure is too great and liable to blow me to smithereens. I can't deal with such pleasure

25

at the minute. Besides, they all signal that final note, I am sacred, comfort me, and I have no reply to that, only questions, concern. Oh God, what was he asking, what was he saying, and why am I so incompetent in knowing? There is something wrong, something very wrong, something to be discovered.

I rush back to my wine and drink as if it were life sustaining medicine, greedily, with far too much drama for my liking. I hold up the bottle and find it is three quarters gone and it is still only mid-evening. Another drink and I'll be fit for nothing but another, and then another until there is only sleep. If I pause now – I'm not fool enough to say stop – I may manage to read something, or at the very least collapse in front of the television and take something in. There might be something worth watching, it's the season for entertainment, television keeping it going almost as well as John and I. But who am I trying to kid. I top up my glass but walk away from the bottle as if I were successfully achieving two things at once.

I think about how else I might have constructed my life. I have resisted the thought for a long time. It seems disloyal. I don't want any other past life, though I would admit the present is not something of which I'd boast. The thought is one of accidents and choices. I see it in imagination like a child's construction game, building new shapes, alternate shapes, one after the other like so many pieces of crazy sculpture. What if I'd moved somewhere else, trained differently, married a different man, where would I be tonight? Everything about me has been built gradually, brick by brick, until I'm fixed in my own woman's twenty-first century. And it might never have been, might never have existed. What if I'd stayed with Frank?

He said he knew the precise moment he went mad – he called it madness. It was a brief moment, a tableau, I suppose, during a life drawing class. He caught sight of the model, standing in a rather bored, classical pose, in a mirror, and his mind instantaneously ran wild with the question as to whether he had really seen her naked or not. From that catastrophic moment he could never believe he was seeing anyone naked – I think he meant it both literally and metaphorically, but he never enlarged on ideas, ambiguity and paradox being everything. I guess that was why he seemed so desperate when we had sex, determined to feel the reality of something that eluded him. He was right of course. Sex is the most consensual act of which we are capable, allowing someone to penetrate you beyond the mirror – a gift so easily squandered. Of course he was using a lot of drugs at the time, but so was everyone.

He was always on edge, always extrovert, unpredictable. He would shout aloud in the street, bizarre slogans, deliberately incomprehensible, determined to shock a public who probably feared violence and were in no way impressed. One day he screamed into the face of a passing teenager, a boy, the insulting sentence: *You're so boring.* His face was contorted, the muscles in his neck extended, the final word elongated, snarled. The boy looked bewildered, humiliated. I'm sure, afterwards, he would have considered numerous responses: hitting out, swearing, maybe even something witty, though probably not, but deep down there would always be the burden of that judgement of unjust exhibitionism. Because, it was, of course, exhibitionism. I always felt he was more inclined to that than madness. It didn't mean that he didn't end up on a cocktail of psychiatric drugs. Of course, all artists want to exhibit and each chooses the effect they wish and work for: to please, to excite, to shock. It's a mistake to settle for – to bore.

He certainly used to bore me with the tedious excitement of his drug life, the stupid details of quantities in a syringe, the absurd vocabulary strictly for those in the know or those who pretended they were, the banal jokes and aggressive humour, the vanity of addiction. He clung to it as if it were an antidote to ageing. How could he be growing old when he had so many of a young man's paradoxes? But he was old, old and burnt out, old way beyond his years, too lazy to countenance a new thought, too lazy to admit he'd let himself down, so he blamed art, or rather the business of art, the need to get shown and make sales. The truth is his drug images were crass, holy relics of false gods, worth nothing.

I loved him though, or at least I had loved him. It took me a long time to work that out, and for a long time I failed to recognize the difference. I used to visit him in hospital and listen to his tirades, for many of which I became the butt. It seemed right to persist. Maybe I felt it was part of my correction, to hold him, try and keep him clean, keep him sane, something to amend for my former impatience and fault. I continued to visit him after I was married, at first in a hostel and then in a bed-sit he called his studio. He couldn't work then, and survived on benefits. I don't know why I continued to sleep with him. I'd like to say it was an act of charity, an act that disgusts me now, but that wouldn't be true. Maybe I was just as intrigued by the mirror as he was. I always assumed that John didn't know, but now I'm not so sure. He certainly knew I went and never discouraged it. He was gentle after my visits, and would touch me tentatively, carefully,

28

as if he understood an old wound was gaping and still liable to pain. He should have put his foot down and made me stop. What would my counsellor say about my infidelity, I wonder, and more to the point, why have I never mentioned it? I'm not supposed to have secrets and yet there are so many.

I go back to the bottle and drink a couple of glasses quickly. My nerves calm.

The wind is strong. It blows in the chimney and in the roof space. I go to the window and look out. In the street the bare cherry trees wave spindly branches. The wind makes screeching noises. This is usually a quiet street, a retreat close to the centre of things. The wind is exposing it. It seems visible in the yellow arcs of the streetlights. Bits of rubbish are blown along. I feel myself, my malformed thoughts, tumble with each piece. Of course, I am drinking, my brain turning to mush. I don't know whether I have started earlier or later than usual. It is after dark and that will do. I am disintegrating into shadow and artificial light, blown to pieces by the elements. If only I could make that feeling complete I might even feel content.

I go back to the Christmas tree, sit on the floor and clutch Joseph's notes to me. The feeling is just absence. He isn't here. He isn't here and I so badly want him here. I want to see my son, share something, a word, a smile, anything. But, of course, he hardly ever was here, so why should I feel his absence? He usually was absent. He was married, a father; he occupied his own world. His absence is nothing out of the ordinary. This absence is how it was. He has been long gone. My mind sinks at the thought. A dull vegetative state overwhelms me. I feel nothing. A small devil's voice whispers that maybe this is restoration, recovery. Yes, he was absent, that is what happens between parent and child, one leaves the other, and the rupture is harsh but heals. But almost immediately a greater voice, the mother voice, goes wild and tears that pretend inner sanctuary to shreds. My child is dead. There is no peace, no solace, no hope. I have no word to describe what I feel. It isn't pain. Pain is one of the non-special senses. Pain tells me where I am, stops me burning myself on fire or ice. What I'm feeling doesn't tell me where I am just where I'm not. And it is special, very special.

I replace his notes beneath the tree. There are telltale damp patches. As so often I have been crying without knowing it. I can't go on like this. It is impossible. I have to make this stop. I return to the dining room, to the wine bottle. I fill my glass. I need courage. I take it to the window, part the curtain and again look out at the wind, or rather the wind's action. My face appears in the glass, lines indistinct, a ghost, a thing devoid of substance. I pull the curtain behind me and I disappear, banished. It was simple. The street is empty. Only the wind occupies it and that is only a sound.

I get down onto my knees and peer out. I imagine snow, a heavy fall, silent, dense and overwhelming. It is the right time for such a fall, such a covering. It would reshape the street, make it glitter, fill it with infinite variety, each crystal unique. I'm sure I remember such falls, such depth, such silence. It's been a long time. Maybe I will never see it again. It will never exist again. A world without snow. An extinction of snow. What would be real then? Everything would have to be imagined, imagined rather than remembered. Of course, so much like snow, imagined rather than remembered. But why make so much about snow? It connects me, I suppose, makes me a little girl again, a little girl now, a girl with dreams, a girl with thoughts. And so it goes. I have to touch something real. I have to know what Joseph meant. I am sacred, comfot me. It is so obvious; I have to go to France. I have to know what happened to my son, that is the choice I have, the choice I take. I need to know that snow exists.

Chapter Four

The first thing I had to do was see Sara and the child. How is it that I have left it so long? I can't deny it felt good to call Vivien and tell her that I couldn't make her pamper session as I had something to do. I whispered that I was moving on, which is true in some respects and a lie in so many others.

When Joseph and Sara were first married they lived in Chiswick in a nice flat, very modern and pristine, something of a show-home, though perhaps more show than home, fine lines of stainless steel and marble, uncluttered and simple, black and white denoting a very contemporary version of truth. At least I saw Joseph then, though rarely Sara. He worked in a small laboratory in Ealing, separate to the company proper which was somewhere in Surrey. He said they liked to keep the science and the sales apart. He was still partly employed by the university then, funded by the company to research their drugs. I presume he was good at what he did because they wanted him to come to them full time. I have never thought about whether he was really happy then, newly married, his career developing, funds apparently no object, because I wasn't happy for him. I assumed he shared my scepticism. But why should that be? We never exchanged notes, not even a sidelong glance.

I have to accept that he loved Sara and still would love Sara. Later, when he went to the company full time – I think it was called Polymed then, later PMP and later still Rennstadt – they had to relocate north. They both termed it relocate. They certainly were not moving, which would imply a permanence that they both deigned to despise. Of course they were right. Joseph ended up in France. A country isn't big enough to hold them now. The market is global – or is it that the globe is a market? I suppose they would have contested the idea of having a home. They had houses, purchases on the road to somewhere that was never quite defined.

I was surprised when Sara stayed in Leeds. My understanding was that she hated it. They moved three times in a year, from a town centre flat to a large house on the edge of a park to a house in a cul-de-sac in an estate of houses. I would have judged the final choice her least favourite, but that is where she stayed and remains. That is where I shall find her. She has little or no reason to welcome me now. Our ties are very loose, though there is Georgia, my granddaughter. I haven't seen her for over six months, not since the funeral. On that day I scarcely spoke to Sara. I don't know how that happened; it just turned out that way. I should be suspicious of such a claim. The unconscious is very good at protecting itself. If two women fail to speak there is something at play. But who was the culprit, me or her, or are we equally culpable. I think our equality is something we struggle with.

The journey here to Leeds was terrible, the train grossly overcrowded, with people sitting on bags between carriages causing the automatic doors to stay open so that there was a constant draught. There was a background buzz of music which sounded like tinnitus, broken by a constant accompaniment of bizarre ring-tones from mobile phones followed by subsequent very public conversation. Just along the aisle someone beat notes from a muffled conga. I took paracetamol as if that could solve the problem. I tried to read but had to go over paragraphs again and again. Eventually I tried to sleep and the sounds in my head coalesced into a single, patterned throb. My mind played tricks, throwing up images of shrunken heads, grossly decorated faces, and shifting pools like multi-coloured lava lamps. That at least afforded some peace.

From the station I have taken a taxi. When I rang to say I was coming Sara didn't offer to collect me. Not surprisingly she was astonished that I was coming at all, and didn't disguise the fact. She even asked me what I wanted. It threw me. I said I just wanted to see Georgia. To that she merely said all right, but added that she wasn't in a position to put me up. I suppose I should have predicted her response, after all, I have never been to the house before.

I could be anywhere, the city centre quickly replaced by wide urban streets, tree lined, backed by small shops. I can't help but try to imagine Joseph striding along the pavement. I think stride is the right word. He had that force and presence, striding and laughing going together somehow. I can hear it now, the way it used to fill up our debates of art and science, form and function, the Arts and Crafts Guild and Bahaus. Such dead conversations now, dead laughter, fouled enthusiasm. Could anything restore it? Only miracles, belief in heaven, lies I cannot commit. And yet I have tutored myself to be resilient. I am on a quest. It has brought me to a place I have never before been, its geography unknown, its airy, tree lined streets a surprise, cleaner and brighter than I expected.

And Joseph was here, striding perhaps where my eye falls, past the estate agents – many estate agents – solicitors' offices, building society offices, banks, mini-markets and the rest, striding because there was a need to arrive, in order to quickly move on – in emotional health, move on. Life was to be consumed in great deserved chunks, the direction of travel upwards, onwards, but to what earthly paradise certainly eluded me, eludes me still. He was brought up to an aesthetic, not the province of money – though money in the bank is always a help – but did I bring him up correctly, did we? How can I ever know? I brought him up to be alive. I failed in that. I failed in the fundamental.

If I'm brutally honest I can't really see him, nothing more than an impression, an image where features and outlines come in and out of focus though never all at once. I summon no more than a recognizable suggestion of him, and can't get closer than that. But if I think of John, it's just the same. If I think of me it's no different. I have an impression, an impression of a face at a taxi window, looking out but seeing inward. (I am obviously not so steeped in grief not to be able to dramatize myself, which is a fault, something to regret.) Sometimes I cry because I can only see an impression, or at least that is the starting point, the thing that leads back to grief. An impression is not good enough, it lets me down. I let him down. There must be more, I must be able to draw more from myself, demand more, achieve more. All of the time I'm looking to find him. He can't be all lost, not completely. I should have taken more account.

I know I should rehearse what I will say to Sara, try to think of something that will make a good impression. Impressions matter to her. She is the daughter of a small scale business-man father and office-administrator mother, who like to boast of their material success, which Sara does too. She was brought up in Streatham, South London, and has a degree in business and finance. She likes themed parties, for instance getting all of the men to wear tuxedo and bow-tie, or having everyone bring a gift of amber, most people opting for beer and wine, but others pieces of jewellery or sunrise prints – though no one's income stretched to insects in resin, as far as I recall. Her friends are beautiful, cheerful and polite. There are no misplaced, reckless souls haunted by demons and addictions, though they are far from prudish, drink to excess and exchange vulgar jokes, which will certainly cease when they all become parents. Their talk then will be of birth-plans and breasts, then nurseries and schools, ambition and success, and so it will go, immune from history if they are lucky, if they continue to be lucky. But that doesn't tell me what to say to her, doesn't prepare the ground at all. It only reminds me why the ground is so difficult, why the paths between us are so broad.

At the funeral she was smartly dressed and angry, an attractive, impassioned widow. I could see the anger in her demeanour. It surprised me. I didn't expect it. Judging by her tone on the telephone she is still angry. It suggests something new about her and being new something better. But is that right? If she is angry for herself then it is unforgivable, but if she is angry because her husband was so young, too young, his death too strange, then there is something commendable in that, something the mother should respect and rejoice in. I know what she will say though – I am angry because my child is an infant. Everything is passed to the children with them. Every self-seeking, selfish act is committed in the name

36

of the children. The children must inherit a benign, trouble free, health and safety world. That is the world constructed for them, its inadequacies and exploitation glossed over; a world without history where only fashion counts. Well, I'm sorry, but the world will spurn and kick at such sanitation and in the end let you down, badly let you down. What will I say to her? How on earth can I begin?

The driver has been speaking and I haven't responded. He must think me incredibly rude, but I'm not, I was pre-occupied, thinking of the encounter to come. I apologize and he says some more, whether repeating himself or not I don't know. I don't understand his accent. I'm not at all sure what he's saying to me. I think to apologize again and say I'm hard of hearing. The idea is amazing. Why would I think to hide behind an imaginary ailment? I laugh and very honestly tell him that I didn't quite understand his accent. My laughter is sweet and flirtatious, laughter I have denied myself for so long. Now it is just to get me out of a hole. It makes me feel guilty, as if I'm letting someone down. Nevertheless he laughs in return, good-naturedly, turns his head to speak more directly to me, slows his voice and asks me if this is my first time, first time in the city. I don't think that is what he was asking me. He's moved on, thought better of it, and settled for the easily answered. Yes, this is my first time. I tell him that my son lived here. The past tense hangs between us, an obvious question mark. He is too professional to be caught out like that. He tells me how much the city has changed and how it is scarcely recognizable. I feel he is trying to soften my disappointment. There is something pleasing in that. For him the job just gets harder. There used to be two rush hours, he laughs, but now they meet

37

in the middle and there's just one. But, he adds, it's always been a great city. I'm sure he's offering that loyalty for my benefit, to justify the fact that my son came here. I feel I should respond but before I can he tells me that we are nearly there, just up and round somewhere, place names that mean nothing to me.

We are in an estate of large, brick houses, all slightly different, separate and unaligned, individual and yet similar enough to stand side by side. Sara will be comfortable with this, the proximity and distance of neighbours, the comparable wealth, the distinct yet shared existence. Or rather, I assume she will be comfortable with this. I am making judgements about her. The taxi pulls up in front of one of the houses. There are no hedges or fences, no marked boundaries, just patches of green, space before the next house and the one following that. The front of the house is paved with diagonally laid bricks. The house is on ground much higher than the road, as are all of the houses. There is a short steep drive to a double-garage. There is a large vehicle parked there, a Land Rover or Jeep, or something similar.

I pay the driver, tipping him generously, perhaps to make up for my inattention, take his proffered card, and then stand for a while simply looking at each of the houses in turn. They speak of a shared lifestyle: similar style cars, simple lawns with narrow empty borders – life is obviously too busy to be a serious gardener – and the same leaded windows and Georgian doors. I am sure the life must be good.

Sara opens the door and steps out onto the paved bricks, looks me up and down, which she always does, and then gazes at me without speaking. Georgia follows, a toddler, immediately comic and appealing, playing a game for herself which must be musical statues. I address myself to the child. "What a big girl you are now," stating the obvious that she is bigger than the last time I saw her; the obvious that it is some time since I saw her. She ignores me and continues her game, moving and stopping, her expression blanked at each halt.

"I didn't think you would really come," Sara says, her tone and expression hostile, unforgiving.

I don't understand. We always played a game of politeness, asking about each other's health and well-being, masking our antipathy and lack of mutual understanding. We have never openly disagreed, not that I remember. Normally I submit to being looked up and down, subject myself to talk of house furnishings, pretend to be flattered by questions of taste and decoration and in turn make appreciative noises about new acquisitions, then ask about her parents, the business-man and his administrator wife, and when really stuck her brothers, the accountants, both probably crooked, one certainly.

Today she is openly disagreeable. I should applaud it if I understood it. Presumably no longer having Joseph to please she can openly declare her dislike of me. It should be tempting to respond to the challenge, fight my corner and tell the wife how narrow and lacking I find her, but I can't. Perhaps it's a generational thing to be polite to the bitter end, or I can't really countenance being left to fend for myself in this lived-in but deserted estate, or maybe I'm finished with it. What's the point? He is dead to both of us, we needn't fight over his remains. I willingly concede. After all Sara has Georgia, a piece of him, the name strange and contemporary to my ears, the child beautiful to the eye.

"I should have come much earlier," I concede, "seen

my granddaughter, seen you. I've been preoccupied by it all. I'm sorry."

"I wouldn't expect it."

"But I should . . . want to."

Something like a smile crosses her lips, something bitter, hurtful. I guess she ran my incompetent, inefficient words together and came up with a joke, hence the dubious amusement. She turns away, says something to Georgia and together they go back to the door, hand in hand, mother and daughter, dressed alike, jeans and knee boots, fur lined, fur cuffed, and short neatly cut bolero jackets. The child is older than her years, the mother younger, both girls, not toddler and woman. In Victorian times Sara would have been expected to stay in black, just the one colour, for at least a year, after which she could introduce another colour and then after eighteen months a further colour, bereavement following a strict code. She would also have been expected to spend her days contemplating on his memory. Of course we are post-modern today and grieve individually.

I personally would benefit from a rule-book. The feeling is too big without. I don't know where to start, can conceive of no end. Of course men were expected to return to work where, according to Adam Smith *society and conversation are the most powerful remedies for restoring the mind to tranquillity*. I have read manuals and textbooks, but get no closer to peace, a peace I deny, a peace I distrust. Of course, for the Victorians even such prescribed mourning was only available for those with the money to purchase it. I'm sure Sara could buy some of it, her designer jeans at least could be black. Am I really so old fashioned? Naturally, when I want to be.

Sara ushers Georgia indoors, turns slowly, acting a

part I don't understand, portraying a grief outside of my vocabulary – despite my reading – and coldly says: "As you are here you'd better come in."

The invitation is so niggardly I hesitate. Should I simply apologize, without knowing for what, and make my exit? That is surely what Sara wants. She doesn't want me across her threshold. But if I go now how do I ever enter Georgia's life again? Up until now I have given it no thought, been a particularly ineffectual grandparent, leaving the field to the overindulgent couple from Streatham, but now faced with its closure I feel a sense of panic. I don't want to be excluded from her life. She is all I have, the very last breath of me. "Yes," I say, scarcely disguising the appeal in my voice. "Yes, I'd like to come in."

Sara goes ahead leaving the door open. I follow, knowing this is a hollow, empty welcome. I am being tolerated, not invited: I have to follow of my own accord, not be led.

I follow Sara through a spacious hallway, where there is a stairway leading up with a wooden spoke banister, through double doors leading into a lounge, into the back of the house where there is a large square kitchen with a central island, the work surface covered in jet black marble. To one side of the kitchen there is a conservatory with rattan furniture and large succulents, to the other, continuous with the kitchen, a play area with large toys, a small lavender coloured, cloth settee and bean bags. She gestures for me to sit in there. The invitation seems needlessly cruel. There is a man sitting on the settee. I hesitate, but then go where directed. He immediately stands and offers to shake my hand, an embarrassed, spontaneous gesture. He is taller than Joseph, fair haired, attractively suffused with redness, his skin imperfect, stippled with dormant freckles, his features rounded, the overall effect one of softness. I should instantly dislike him but don't. I don't take his hand but smile, weakly, in just the way I should. He scoops up some papers from the settee, takes his jacket from the back of it, and says he'll go, says it in a way that makes it clear he is vacating the room, the house, not that he has to go. Does he want me to be grateful? Well, I am. If I am tempted to manufacture some doubt as to the nature of their relationship it is dashed by the intimacy of their kiss on parting. Much to my horror and distress it is redolent with symbolic good luck, as are his parting words and the farewell glance he gives me. There is also an added note of pity for me. God knows what Sara has said about me, but the man has obviously concluded that I'm maybe not as bad as has been suggested.

I sit where he was sitting and wait. The room looks out onto the garden. It isn't large, and is surrounded by a creosote fence. In the centre is a trampoline, and littered around it are a tricycle, go-cart, and other bits and pieces that I can't really work out.

Sara brings a jug of filter coffee and a plate of biscuits. She can either sit by me or flop onto a bean-bag. She refuses either and brings a stool from the island in the kitchen and sits on that. She is much higher than me, surveying me.

I say: "I was surprised when you stayed in Leeds."

She looks at me sharply, weighing up my words, then visibly relaxes, relieved by something. "Steven you mean. He's kind, a nice guy, good with Georgia. Who knows?"

"Yes, he looked kind," I concede, suffering it, his being good with Georgia. "But no, I wasn't meaning that, him I mean. In general, I thought you didn't like it that much."

"What choice do I have?" she snaps, looking at me darkly, as if I am culpable. "Do you think selling this would buy me a doll's-house in London?"

"It's a nice house."

"Yes, it's a nice house," she says, leaving something else unsaid but apparent.

I don't know how to continue. To go on will draw me into their world, man and wife, practicalities of their life together, something that at the moment seems as intimate as sex. "I presume Joseph left you well provided. I mean, he was very practical, and you with numbers."

Quite rightly she looks horrified. How could I have said, you with numbers? I make it sound like a complaint, a physical illness rather than an attribute. She stares at me incredulously. Finally she utters: "No, Joseph did not leave me well provided for as I'm sure you know."

I don't know what to say, but I can't leave it where it is. "Surely he would have had life assurance, benefits from work."

She glares at me, and I can't tell whether she might burst into tears or laughter, both look possible and likely. Finally she gives a peremptory smile, slips off her stool and walks out into the garden where Georgia has already gone and is sitting on her tricycle. Sara goes right to her and kneels down in front of her, the coffee cup held in both hands, warming them I suppose. It is a cold blustery day, the wind strong enough to be heard. There is something deliberate about kneeling down to the child and speaking, something symbolic. It eradicates other thought for her, I feel sure of it.

I find myself thinking that she is a good mother. I have never seen her angry, only indulgent. Is it fair to complain about indulgence? So she has never entertained

43

large thought, considered a world beyond the confines of her narrowness, but I don't suppose it has ever been her intention to wish it harm. She is shallow, materialistic, judgemental but not bad. She falls short of the mark, but maybe I'm the one who has it wrong with my redundant, worn-out ideals, my forsaken dreams. I should have given thought to that, been less inclined to judge, letting mother bias get in the way. It's hardly criminal to be petty in this petty world. I of all people should have learned that people should be allowed to live the life they want to live without the interfering judgement of an ousted mother. I should ask her forgiveness, though I have never been one to forgive myself.

I remember when my mother asked me to see my father, and she cried at my refusal, that I was heartless to her, dismissive of her facile desire to want to make peace. I didn't want to make peace, put the past to rest, my anger assuaged. I wanted it to go on and on, the feeling of derision, the desire for revenge. He had made her life hell, a brutalized hell, a shadow of a life, and at the end she wanted absolution, a world made right. Well, I wasn't the one to do it, to give in. I ridiculed her, told her that her forgiveness stank of hypocrisy, tried to make her see that she didn't have to do it. I said the dying don't deserve forgiveness just because they are dying. They should take our contempt to the grave. She didn't challenge me, just asked me to do it for her. She pointed out that Vivien was there all of the time, and it was only right that I should be too. I despised Vivien's easy, thoughtless peace. I refused again and again, but in the end I simply ran out of refusals and couldn't resist her overtures anymore.

I remember when I went in that he nodded, acknowledging the import of the moment, as I guess we both saw

44

it. And in that nod there was something about wanting but not demanding forgiveness, even a desire to be understood, which I had never considered. His actions, particularly when they were younger, my father and mother, were beyond reason.

I looked at him sitting in his chair drowning in his own body, his own fluids filling his lungs, yet trying to talk, entertain me with his resilience, and I thought, I want more. I want insight and reasons. I want you to explain what lies behind this. I wanted him to decode the whole human condition – its violence and aggression, its impatience and waste, its acts of charity and dissent, its labours. Instead he struggled on with bland observations about the weather, and accounts of the minor trials of other people's lives. I left feeling that the answer to the mystery will always be denied us because at the point of knowing the mind is blanked, wisdom annulled for lack of oxygen, clean air unpolluted by sickness.

Did I manage to forgive him, love him even? Certainly there was no forgiveness, but there was more love than I'd felt remotely possible. It was an abstract, humanitarian love. Maybe, after all, that was wisdom, his parting message. When he died I was glad. My mother remarried shortly after, a much younger man and was very happy for a little while, a decade or so, when she died as well, and I don't recall that he was ever mentioned again. I always had the sneaking suspicion that she had forgiven herself for something, but for what, and how that worked, I never did understand, and now never can. We either ask too many questions or too few, or simply the wrong ones.

I watch mother and daughter for a while and then go out to join them, wanting to say something positive to both. I'm sure Sara can hear my approach, besides which

45

Georgia watches me all of the way, but she makes no acknowledgement of my presence.

"The garden must be lovely in the summer," I say, "lovely for Georgia to play."

Sara stands up, turns to me and calmly says: "I am in prison here. That's what you want to know, isn't it? I am trapped, and there's nothing I can do."

"I don't understand Sara."

She considers her reply and begins to speak, but any words she might have said fail and instead she purses her lips and shakes her head.

In some ways it is a more legitimate show of grief, but I am not reassured by it. "Why didn't you go to France with him if you dislike it so much here?"

"You don't know, do you?"

"Don't know what?"

"Joseph left us. Joseph went to France with another woman."

I can't make sense of the scale of what has been said. I simply look at Sara as if I have been caught out in some acutely embarrassing situation, found naked in the street, not in a dream. Why am I so often naked in company, I asked my counsellor, who smiled, certain that I was conning him. But this is real, demands something of me that I am incompetent to supply. I don't understand why Sara should seem to be displaying some satisfaction at this moment. Is it one of the worst of human traits to be quietly entranced by misfortune? Do I see myself in that? I would hope not, but can't deny the possibility. I have no ability but to further the conversation, the confession.

"I don't understand," I say, aware of the absurdity of my words. "He was working. He went to France for the company he was working with."

46

"He left work a year ago, no, more, more than a year. How time flies when you're having fun."

"Don't Sara," I say, eyeing her carefully, examining that self-deprecating cynicism. "You don't have to say things like that."

She looks incensed, outraged that I should have an opinion. Perhaps she is right. But I am the mother; I am not immune. "I don't understand," I repeat, feeling something wrench within me without understanding it, without being able to say where that feeling rests. The body tears as the mind decomposes. "He wouldn't leave Georgia," I insist, saying something aloud that I know has to be true.

I look towards her. She is entertaining herself, trying to peddle her way across the heavy grass, trying to gather momentum that she doesn't have. In my mind's eye she is not capable of entertaining herself. I only see her demanding attention, demanding that any momentum she needs is supplied. I am guilty of ludicrous insinuation and judgement. But would I not also insist that there are Tennant – and Shore, never completely losing myself – genes that are better controlled, less selfish. It's all nonsense. I'm just bitter at my exclusion, at the prized position the other grandparents have, Sara's domination.

Sara is looking at me, weighing up my gaze on her daughter, and there is something akin to pity in her expression. "He stopped being himself. He stopped some time back. He got like you, serious and pious." Somehow she has managed to say it without rancour.

"Is that how you see me?" I ask without excitement. She shrugs. "It's not the whole picture," I go on in the same tone. I can see protest in her features. "I know, it doesn't matter. Of course it doesn't matter. Not now, but all the same, just so you know."

47

"You never made any effort to make me feel comfortable."

"That isn't true."

"I know I'm right and nothing will make me think otherwise."

There is something petulant in her self-assertion, something that suggests that being right is more important than any other consideration, including sympathy, charity, even bland pity. Surely it isn't so simple. Does she not consider the line drawn between us when she looks me up and down, from head to toe, judging me: does she not see the distance she creates when she dresses my granddaughter like a teenage model; does she not see the reversal she causes when she makes my son into an arrogant, trivial fool. Except he got like me, serious and pious, and presumably with secrets as well. Of course Sara, we each have our secrets, our dreadful dark remains. And you are telling me that Joseph had his. He went to France with another woman. He had left his job. How can anyone ever be right when there is so much hidden, undisclosed, kept grudgingly secret?

"I don't want to make you think anything, Sara."

"I know I'm right."

"Yes, you said. I'm sorry."

"Joseph could have done more. Between you, you should have made me feel more comfortable."

"I don't understand," I respond, aware that I keep saying it, aware that this time it has no meaning.

"You had it between you, something you hung on to, something that you kept together."

"He was my son."

She frowns, though not with temper but displeasure. "So, of course there was no life assurance, no benefits

48

from work, because he wasn't paying, hadn't paid for eighteen months. So I'm sorry Mrs Tennant, they said, there is nothing for you."

"I'm sorry. I didn't realize."

"Of course you didn't realize. How could you know? Unless he confided in you. Did he? Did he tell you what the hell got into him that he would treat us like this?"

"No he didn't confide in me. I don't think he has confided in me since he was a little boy."

"I'm sorry but I don't care. I know what you must be feeling, but I can't help that. Do you understand? He has done too much, too much harm."

"Yes, of course."

"What choice have I got? My parents said to go back to them. It's an option, but I can't do that. I can't live with them again. I could try and sell this and find something, but this is mine, mortgaged to the hilt but mine. And there's Steven. You never know. So I work, engage very expensive childcare and get by. It isn't the life I had planned, not the one Joseph promised, but that's how it is."

"I could help out."

"No, no you can't."

"She is my granddaughter."

"She? She is okay, fine, doesn't really remember Joseph, doesn't remember you."

"Are you excluding me?"

She considers for a moment, no more, her mind quick, decisive, alert. She shakes her head. "No, I'm not," she says, her voice lowering, "I don't have that complete right. But you'll always be Joseph's mother."

I nod my agreement, without knowing what I've agreed to. To play the wicked witch probably, though more likely

49

to play nothing at all. The child will be hers, created of like materials, dressed in her garments, seeing the world through the lens of her eyes, free to be her. Well, Mrs Tennant – our borrowed identities have made so much of us – I am sure that the child will have something to say about that. There are secrets that are so large they refuse to lie dormant. The child will wonder about herself, want to fit her jigsaw pieces onto the board, and when she finds that so many don't fit, she will ask questions. You might have readymade answers, but she'll see through those, see through to something that has to be opened, excised like a festering wound. It will never be enough for her to know that her father left. It isn't enough.

"Did they say anything at work about why Joseph left?"

"I spoke to some of the people he worked with but understandably they didn't want to say anything. I imagine they were too embarrassed or too frightened."

"Frightened?"

"Yes, frightened, abandoned wife with abandoned child asking why, wouldn't you be frightened? Who would want to get caught up in something as pathetic as that? His close friend Gareth said that he thought he was bothered by some research grant, but I should really talk to his line manager, and that Amy who he loved to work with, and I bet he did, said she didn't know anything and I should talk to his line manager."

"And did you?"

"Did I what?"

"Talk to his line manager."

"Yes, of course. Mr Davidson was very polite, sympathetic and useless. He didn't see how he could help over a former employee. He did say that he was personally very disappointed when Joseph left. He was very good at his job. That made me feel so much better knowing that Joseph was good at his job."

"It's strange that no one should speak to you."

"Is it? I don't think I would want to say to someone's wife that they knew all along that he was involved with another woman and planned to leave and go away with her. Funnily enough, I don't find that strange at all."

"But presumably they'd been your friends too."

"No, not really. They came to parties in the house, but I wouldn't say they were my friends. They were the people Joseph worked with, but that changed, changed all of the time."

Georgia begins to cry, seemingly frustrated by her feeble tricycle that she has been dragging rather than riding along the lawn. Sara smiles, amused by her child's temper, and responds to her immediately. The child wants pushed, wants speed and excitement. Sara obliges, making engine sounds, the sound of cars skidding, braking, going fast. I am frozen, my hands numb with cold, my legs shaking. Cold is the same as fear, produces the same effects. I remain completely still, rendered inert, watching mother and child at play, somehow the two of them immune to either cold or fear. If I was a proper grandmother I would be the one doing the pushing, talking her up as I did, making big of her, celebrating her amazing and sensational success as driver, pilot, or whatever we might decide together. I'm hopeless. My toddler language has all dried up. It is reserved for memory, for a boy who was destined to abandon wife and child. I should be ashamed, ashamed in so many ways, and maybe if I could feel, I would be. I rub my hands wanting to stimulate my reluctant circulation. I must cut a poor figure just standing, watching them at their play, a figure who has strayed into the wrong place.

I have played before, played for hours, enacting so many imagined realities, games of sleeping and stalking tigers, crawling, prowling and leaping through all the rooms of the house, encountering hostile plains and savage hunters, though we always escaped and came through even after separation, meeting again in the dining room, on the landing, somewhere in our jungle house. But now that beautiful reunion can't happen. I'm sure he was never too old for it. Surely I should be able to take his child on the same journey; though of course the mother would forbid it, and perhaps she'd be right. Joseph ended up dead, the hunters triumphant after all.

Georgia has grown bored with her tricycle and wants to bounce on the trampoline, but Sara has to bounce with her. Sara obliges without question. They hold hands and giggle, at first like bathers bobbing in waves, and then like acrobats, rising ever higher, sleek as two arrowheads. After a while Sara calls for a rest but Georgia will not allow it. She wants to bounce ever more violently. Sara doesn't refuse. It seems she never does. Why do I find fault in that? Why not pleasure in it, the primacy of the young, given the attention we all deserve. Surely the world that loves its young is a good world. The trouble is I don't trust it. It is like so much art, fashion before function. Fashion before everything. Besides which, I am heavy sore. I go up to the trampoline and stand there trying to enliven my expression with the character of an audience, a well satisfied, well pleased audience of one.

Sara looks at me as if I've outstayed my welcome, the enjoyment she is feeling withering on her face. I suppose I bring her bouncing figure banging back to earth, the terrible reminder that she may be bouncing like this, alone, for many years to come – though there is always Steven, someone I logically should be warming to. "You're a wonderful mother, Sara," I call, wanting to reverse that declension.

"Well, she is my child," she snaps breathlessly, her tone quietly inflamed.

I nod my agreement, my acceptance of her claim and all that it means, and all that stems from it, the flowering it suggests. "I wish things were different," I say.

I'm not sure she has heard me, nor indeed am I at all sure that I wanted her to. She releases Georgia's hands, seizes her beneath the armpits and swings her up and brings them both down onto their backsides. Georgia shrieks with pleasure and demands to do it again. Sara deserts her for a moment and crawls to the edge of the trampoline, to the opening in the safety net where I am waiting. Her face is flushed, the skin enriched, her torso heaving. She looks striking: young, attractive, brave and full of need. I want to stroke her face, touch its burning surface but wouldn't commit such an indiscretion. What on earth would she do if I did?

"But things aren't different, Louise, and we have to live with that.

She is lecturing me, measuring her youthful grief against mine and finding mine wanting, wallowing in pity. I can't defend myself. Yes, she outdoes me – except there is Steven and John is nowhere near.

Georgia is demanding Sara's attention, in fact quite quickly seems to be on the verge of a tantrum. "I think you're wanted," I suggest.

"Yes, I am," Sara quietly agrees, and turns on the child

roaring like a roused bear. I leave them to it, their laughter trailing me. I know I should leave a note, something short and to the point, something like, Call me, whenever, but go straight through the house and let myself back out onto the paved drive.

I wander away from the house, knowing that I am not going to be called back. I presume she will see my decision to go as an insult. She'll condemn me for not taking a proper leave of my granddaughter, knowing full well that she doesn't want us to have any such doting relationship. For her own part she'll be beneficent. She can do without my offices, good or bad; they leave her cold. She will not see my leaving as the desperate escape of a disintegrating woman. How many shocks is a body able to withstand? I feel certain that I have been mortally wounded. The last thing that sustained me is leaking from me like blood. All I can do is lie to myself or call Sara a liar. I can't reappraise my son, change my relationship to him on the strength of his outrage to her, but how do I hang onto the character I have made him, the one he has to be? I wish I had never come to this God forsaken place, but what then?

For the moment I can't think with any coherence. I just want to go home. I'm grateful for the taxi driver's card. I didn't take it with any thought. Without it I'd be lost on this estate forever. Thank God I brought my phone, which is not something I routinely do. He says he'll be twenty minutes or so. I stand on a corner, impervious to everything.

The taxi driver asks whether my trip was successful or not. I tell him that it was all right, and surprise myself with my willingness to assume niceties. Of course it wasn't successful. I have learned terrible things. My son

54

is a monster. But that cannot be. There has to be a mistake that I can decipher. The taxi driver announces that we are coming to the station and I tell him I've changed my mind. I want to be taken to the offices of Rennstadt.

Chapter Five

The taxi driver laughs and calls over his shoulder that it would be so easy to be lost, which is an announcement that startles me. It is like being woken up, surprised into reality. His face is in the mirror, or at least its centre, the heart of it, mouth, nose and eyes. He is still laughing, his swarthy cheeks raised, his eyes crinkled and his mouth open. He is laughing because it would be so easy to be lost, but then he is a pathfinder so presumably immune and therefore amused. Should I tell him that he is exactly right and I am lost, that his taxi driver intuition has picked it up correctly? But the conversation seems too strange to countenance. I simply shrug, indicating my lack of understanding. He laughs more loudly. He means the gridiron roads, all the same, the endless repetition of business units, set back from the road behind aluminium fences. He remembers it when it was marsh and woodland and people used to walk their dogs, play football and the like. Now there isn't a person to be seen, no one to ask a single direction. He has known people drive around for hours looking for unit A1 or ZK, whatever it was, and never find it yet. So, I respond, if we see men with beards we should rescue them. He is delighted. He laughs more than necessary. I am delighted too. I have made a friend.

Luckily he does know his way and pulls off the main road onto a narrower side road and then again into a quadrangle, a car park surrounded on all sides by various office units. As far as I can tell there isn't a single free space. As a car user the taxi driver points it out, the lack of space, how it is the same in all of these units. He doesn't know how people cope. Of course he is asserting his freedom. He suggests it could spoil your whole day. I smile appreciatively. He's right, it could spoil the whole day. I ask him which one is Rennstadt. He indicates the building in front of which he has pulled up, frowning slightly as if it was obvious. He is a professional and something of a friend so he would naturally pull up outside. He tells me that the building also has the offices of a media company and the offices of the cancer network. He is something of a tourist guide, though whether he is impressed by the city's development or disgusted by it would be hard to say. He is a taxi driver so simply chronicles it, the change, the increasing difficulty of getting about, the shifting world in front of his eyes. My world changes in more hidden ways. I am lost; he is still driving.

I get out, go to his window and ask him what I should do. He looks at his watch. Do I have any idea how long I will be? I shake my head. I want to tell him that I don't even know what I intend to do. I suppose I should question this need for an ally. What am I doing? I know it is something about Joseph, but I'm not clear what. Is it just to be somewhere he was, or do I have questions, real, grown-up enquiries unspoiled by grief? I shrug again and smile. I can see it in my mind's eye, the pertness, the suggestion of being a bit scatter-brain. He will like that. He tells me he's going to park up and have his sandwiches and coffee, indicating a lunch-box and flask on the passenger seat. I just need to ring. I find it comforting to have him close by.

I'm sure the building originally had a number as the

taxi driver suggested but now it's Phoenix House. On some plan somewhere, whoever owns all this and rents it out, the number will still be there, income tallied against it, but in the cold light of a blustery day, it's Phoenix House. How many buildings must also be called Phoenix House? Joseph was part of this world. Can I blame Phoenix House, and all the family of Phoenix Houses, for making my son bluff and ambitious, shallow and saddled with the refrain *entertain me*? Is that why I am here, to hurt myself with harsh realities? Phoenix House! I despise it.

The occupants are listed on a nameplate as if it were the chambers of a group of solicitors or doctors, decent, respectable professionals, aiding the local community. Rennstadt probably have offices and laboratories in Shanghai, Kentucky, Abidjan, Sydney. They'll certainly be bigger than any country, making global citizens of its workforce, or so they will believe and they'll be flattered by it, bought off by it. They are certainly not here to aid the local population. The world is becoming too small for all of us. What sort of place will it be with no more secrets, no discoveries and no surprises. A place of gimmicks. A place of decline.

The entrance is spacious and bare, a large single pot-plant to the left, a reception desk to the right, two large, abstract prints on the two side walls, fluid splodges of orange and yellow, the back wall with large open double-doors giving access to two lifts. Once upon a time the splodges might have demanded interpretation, posed questions about ways of seeing, of perception itself. The experiment would have been seen as an exploration, a journey into the meanings of surface and dimension. Now they are wallpaper. The end of discovery is wallpaper.

The plant assumes symbolic significance placed alone in such barren, empty space. What is it saying? There is light here, because it grows, thrives. Someone obviously supplies the water and nutrients. Life is cared for, so we must be in safe hands. Of course it could simply be very stingy decoration indeed. Surely if all these companies clubbed together I could be greeted by a jungle. As it is I simply have to negotiate my way past the receptionist.

She is young, smartly dressed, attractive, with very fine lines. She doesn't speak but gestures through her whole figure that she is giving me her undivided attention. I say the name of the company. I expect to be ushered to the lifts and told which floor, but she looks at me questioningly. I return the gesture. She wants to know whether I am expected. I am too alert to say no, but suggest not exactly. Well, who have I come to see? I smile as if I am a friend of everyone in the company and very casually suggest Gareth or Amy, as if it really wouldn't matter which. She asks if she can have their surnames. In that moment I don't know their surnames. Of course I know Gareth's, he was Joseph's friend for years, but it has gone completely out of my head. I try to convey the absurdity of that to the receptionist, the fact that I could forget the surname of a pal. She suggests that she'll ring up and see if anyone knows who I mean. When she has entered the number she asks me who she should say is here. I don't want to give my name, knowing it will debar me in some way, but I'm too slow to work out an alternative and acquiescently say, Mrs Tennant, Louise, Louise Tennant.

When the phone is answered she turns away from me and lowers her voice. I hear her say that there is a Mrs Tennant in the lobby, looking for a Gareth or an Amy. She makes them sound like objects, potential purchases.

I smile at her, acknowledging the flimsiness of the information I have given. There is more conversation and then she puts down the telephone. She informs me that they are going to make inquiries and ring back. She continues with something else. She has decided that I am obviously not a significant client and she doesn't have to be anything more than polite with me.

There are no seats in what she calls the lobby, which strikes me as an accurate but pompous term, so I stand. I feel awkward and exposed in that space. I am now in context with the plant and the paintings. I am now significant. My signification works at other than eye level. I have furnished a name, Mrs Tennant, Mrs Louise Tennant, the first name asserted as if demanding a former identity. I am Mrs Tennant but I am also Louise; as Louise I too was young, an artist, and I saw many things and I did many things, so don't misread me. I pattern my expression, suggesting my boredom with the lobby and its contents. I want to impress on her that I am a busy woman of business. That is what she will be used to. I should have played that role from the start. It might have got me through.

The phone rings. She listens without speaking, replaces it on its stand and then tells me that they have made inquiries but can't help with a Gareth or an Amy, then shrugs and suggests that it would have helped if only I'd had their surnames. I ask for a moment and go outside. There is nothing for it but to ring Sara. She is naturally surprised and uncomfortable hearing my voice. With understandable curtness she demands to know what I want now. The now seems unnecessary, implying that I'm regularly demanding something, which is wrong in every way. I ask for Gareth and Amy's full names. She naturally wants to know why. There should be no reason not to say it's because I want to see them, but I feel there is something to be kept secret about it. I very lamely say I can't remember, that's all, but as they were his friends I'd like to recall them. It is feasible, the mother reminiscing. By this time Sara has obviously given it some thought and not managing to work out any objection snaps out Gareth Gate and Amy Tomlin.

I return as if flush with memory, my lackadaisical mind put to rights. I would like to see Dr Gate or Dr Tomlin. Again she rings up and this time is told immediately that neither is available. She puts the phone down again and I ask her why they are not available. She looks at me with a certain degree of irritation. She has no idea. She is only one of the ground floor staff, not a member of Rennstadt or any other company, therefore she can't say. I adopt what I believe to be a penitential look and ask her, if she doesn't mind, whether she could ask whether Mr Davidson is free. Once again she rings up. This time the information is unequivocal. Mr Davidson has moved to the London office. She looks at me as if she expects me to produce another name.

I wish I could. In coming here I have made a compact with myself that I expect something from it, even if I don't know what it is. There is something impoverished about going away empty-handed. But there is nothing else for it but to leave. I thank her, aware that my voice betrays a thickness of emotion, my disappointment and hurt surfacing. She recognizes it and tells me she's sorry. That indefinite apology heartens me. It's somehow pleasant that she's sorry at my dissatisfaction, whilst neither protecting, defending nor condemning anyone else, simply sorry that I feel as I do. I purse my lips, giving that telltale smile which admits that there are things going on, human depths, and go back outside.

I stand on the steps for some time, reluctant or even unable to take an immediate leave. The strangeness of this workaday place bothers me. There is so much evidence of people, but no proof. There are numerous cars, some blocking in others, cars and no spaces, but no people. There are rows on rows of connected windows, all tinted, reflecting the buildings opposite, together with the blue sky with its quickly moving trails of watery cloud and the thin, spindly branches of winter trees, but offering no signs or evidence of the people within. The architecture looks out. It is art as function, blending into the landscape, cancelling itself. The people don't exist, Dr Gate and Dr Tomlin unavailable. But why are they unavailable? I am a grieving mother, surely a few minutes of their time would be time well spent. The chances are that I will never stand in this self-referencing space ever again, so I need to make it count. I can't walk away empty-handed. I consider going back to the receptionist and pleading my case, openly telling her my history, my hurt, my need to hear from Dr Gate and Dr Tomlin, but she is only a member of the ground floor staff so I guess wouldn't sanction any breaking and entry. But, of course, that is the answer, criminal trespass.

As I ponder the break-in a group of three women come from the car park and pass me. They have that air of being just and no more in time for a meeting, their conversation loud and business-like. One of them goes to the receptionist and obviously signs them all into the building, whilst the other two go for the lift. At this point they are joined by a fourth who rushes in and catches them just before the lift closes.

I consider brazening my way in, going right up to the reception, signing my name and taking the lift as well. But of course, I'd be recognized, besides which I lack all of the supporting paraphernalia, an open coat and scarf, a brief-case tucked under my arm, a suit. I'm dressed for travel, black jeans, slipper shoes, mustard coloured coat. I look a different part altogether, though wear it well. Why is that? Why do I bother? Is it habit or diehard vanity? I presume it's the latter. How dreary I am, my grief a sham, my hurt a posture. But a voice sears through the bleakness: It is illegal to go naked, to pine in the gutter, to howl. I would be pumped full of drugs if that were the case. I don't want to be out of my mind other than in my own crazy, riddled way, the right side of the mirror.

As these thoughts go through my mind another group of women – again four, sharing cars obviously, parking a premium – make their way to the entrance. They could be the first group again they are so alike. I look at my watch and pace as if I'm waiting for someone. I have to look as if I have purpose; only purpose is without suspicion, loitering always suspect. One of them says hello. I am accepted as part of the group, a working woman. Why else would any of us find ourselves in such a sterile domain? I watch them cross the lobby, again one of them signing them in, whilst the others call the lift. When the lift doors open I hurry in and make my way to join them, even calling out for them to hold it for me. As the lift doors close behind me I turn and see that the receptionist is looking our way, but whether with any real interest or not I can't discern. I tell myself I should be indifferent to her recognising me. At the worst I can be ejected, but I don't want the scene, the fright, the being laid bare as a grieving obsessive mother. My counsellor would certainly refute that this behaviour is moving on.

The lift stops at the third floor. When I stepped inside one of the women gestured for me to say which floor. She had already pressed for the third. I simply smiled and nodded. On the landing outside the lift are toilets and we all troop in. Being a blustery, wild day we have to check our appearance, put everything back in place. I go into a cubicle and wait, listening for them to go.

Having given the women ample opportunity to go into their meeting I make my way out of the toilet. The landing lets onto another space with a number of doors to either side, all ajar. Straight in front is a partition wall, the upper portion glass, with a set of double doors. The sign beside the door says it is the West Yorkshire Cancer Network. Through the windows I can see a vast open office space covering an entire floor. I can't guess how many people are working here, nor can I imagine what they do. People sit in front of computer screens or mill about, sharing moments away from the desk. There must be so many spaces like this, people in front of screens doing something with data that the artist can't comprehend, I can't comprehend. I go closer to the windows in order to peer in.

I have never been an office worker, not even when I was a student and took summer jobs. I worked in a hospital kitchen. It was in an underground basement, buried beneath London. The place was overrun with cockroaches. Periodically pest control would come and spray gas behind the skirting and thousands of cockroaches would scuttle about, the majority returning to where they came from, apparently unscathed. I remember doing a triptych called *The Pest Controller*, the centre-piece showed a dying man in a grey windowless room. I'd painted in the background in thick oils and then chipped it away and painted over it because I'd seen a documentary that told how Edvard Munch had done that in his painting *The Sick Child*. It described how he'd attacked the canvas and I wanted to imitate that. In the right panel there were faceless mourners standing as rigidly as bowling pins, standing against a veined mauve background. In the left panel there was a figure dressed in protective clothing, his face mask composed of large gaping sockets, spraying gas which is going nowhere but pluming around him, the background magenta. It did very well, earning me excellent marks. I was told it set up thrilling correspondence, the metaphor complex and compelling, the surface rich in detail and reference. I was naturally pleased. Frank said it was derivative and predictable. It pained me to hear that. I didn't know he was mad then, mad with jealousy and ill will. Why do people hurt each other? Is that not the great mystery of life? I remember going to the Tate to see Munch's painting and being shocked that it was different, the background green, not the chipped and scarred surface I'd seen in the film. I didn't realize that an artist would duplicate work. But of course he would, working through obsession until there is some sense to it, however barbaric.

It was over Munch that I stood up to Frank. He was praising *The Scream*, a painting on which Munch had written that it could only have been painted by a madman, a sentiment Frank thoroughly applauded. Very caustically I said that he'd meant it was a failure. Frank despised me for that comment, or maybe for the temerity of it. When John and I saw *The Sick Child* he was wholly appreciative and said it hurt. He was never given to affectation so meant it. He also knew to question why he found it beautiful, but knew it was. We went to see an exhibition of Munch's paintings of workers intended for public spaces, industrial spaces and I knew I was right, *The Scream* was a failure, a madman's painting, however vivid and compelling, and I knew that I had grown up, freed myself, settled into who I wanted to be. Perhaps that's why I slept with Frank again, because it was me doing it, me whole and complete, as much as I could be. It doesn't make it right, but some things can never be made right.

I feel like a dispossessed child, my nose to the glass, peering into a world in which I don't belong. I wouldn't delude myself and deny that the way I feel isn't exactly how I want to feel. I'm playing up to an artist's notion of art. If I'm not careful I'll become as hell-bent and crooked as Frank. I have no hatred of the modern world; my dispute is that it has hurt me grievously. I have no romantic notions of a better world, though once I believed there was one to come. That particular dream has long withered.

Someone comes out of the office, the opening door releasing a sudden bullet of sound. I back away from the window, failing entirely to look as if I had a reason to be there. A young woman says hello and goes into the first room adjacent the office doors, pushing the door wide open. The room turns out to be a kitchen. I can hear her filling and boiling a kettle, then preparing cups. I step by the open door hoping I won't be noticed. I have to get to Rennstadt's offices before someone challenges me. I slip back onto the landing. Tucked away in the corner is a door with a sign that says: Only to be used in the case of a fire. It strikes me as strange that there should be an insistence on using the lift, an unhealthy laziness. I hope it means that the fire-escape allows access to all floors, bypassing any gatekeepers. I go to the door, quickly check that I'm not being watched, and then slip through.

The dark landing gives way to a bright open stairway, uncarpeted, without the apparent luxury of the rest of the building. I run upwards, assuming Rennstadt occupies the upper levels, calculating that the private company will have more finance to spare than the state cancer network and can therefore purchase better views, lofty heights. In fact floors four and five are occupied by Patent Media. Their sign says: Patent Media incorporating Demon and Damask. The mind boggles. What is behind the door? A door is always a wonder. A door separates spaces, separates realities. Every knock at a door is a possibility. Friend or foe? Will something happen, or will everything carry on in the same predictable way. *Demon and Damask* intrigues me. Was it formerly one company or two? And why, with such an intriguing, enterprising name did it have to throw in its lot with Patent Media? Of course patent has a much more business-like, management ring to it. Patent means ownership and control, whereas demon and damask denote black magic and silk. I go right up to the door and put my ear against it. I can't hear anything.

I tell myself to get on. Time might be short. I have to stop acting like a child let loose in a play area. Already a security guard might be looking for me, alerted to my snooping. At the same time I think it highly unlikely. Who am I, after all, just a woman with a day-return ticket. Of course, I'm not so naïve not to realize that I have been let out for the day and despite myself discovering ways to enjoy it. The thought brings me up cold. I pull away from the door and begin to trudge down the stair. To hell with demon and damask, devil and woven cloth, my purpose is serious and pious; Sara is right, serious and pious. I'm better like that. I go downstairs, remove my coat and lay it across the steps so that I look less like a visitor, an intruder, push my fingers through my hair and loosen it, as if that too will make me look plausible and then I go to investigate.

Rennstadt occupies the ground and first floor. The ground floor is restricted access for authorized staff only. The first floor is a quiet maze of offices, a space of filtered, subdued light and hush. The floor is laid with plain, heavy carpet, the walls smooth and lilac, the doors wood grain. All the doors are closed. In Rennstadt people must work privately. I am learning something. Within the same building, the same risen from the ashes economy, there are many ways of working. In Rennstadt everyone must be deserving of their own unique space; maybe scientists like artists work better confined. I never explored it with Joseph. It was only very occasionally that I ever witnessed him at work in a laboratory. He was happy among experiments, with equipment. He got like me. I reside in my makeshift, domestic studio and engage with gouache, silk-screen and weave, yearning to recast reality in a new and startling way, though hopelessly failing time and again, persevering without understanding why.

Perhaps Joseph was always like me, more like me than either of us knew or would have admitted. Because of it we sometimes fell out, too alike to attract, but could never dispense with each other, too alike not to attract, two basic elements that together made something more complex. I'm sure he could have told me so much more with all of his knowledge of particles, compounds, elements, catalysts and the rest. Somehow in all of that we fitted. Now I don't know; now I'm breaking down into dissolvable salts, my basic shape at risk. I am lost. Even the taxi driver could see that.

Each door is labelled either for person or function: store-room, photocopying-room, Mr Davidson. He might be in London but his office remains. I try the door but it's locked. At that moment someone comes out onto the corridor. I call out that I'm just going to get a drink, as if I've just come from someone's office, a guest, comfortable in the role. I step back along the corridor and pour myself a glass of water from an iced drinks dispenser. I say hello to a girl who passes, a tall, slim girl wearing a patterned jumper and jeans, her expression dreamy or maybe suspicious. Her reply is inaudible and she carries on. I resume where I stopped. Two doors later there is the office of Dr G. Gate. I consider it but move on. A further three doors and I come to Dr A. Tomlin. I reason that a woman will be more understanding, despite the fact that I've never met Amy, whereas Gareth I have, umpteen times. He has stayed in my house, our house, the house of John, Louise and Joseph, currently occupied by Louise alone.

I try the door and it opens, but the light isn't on and there is no one inside. I go in anyway and close the door behind me. The room isn't particularly spacious but is comfortable. It consists of a desk with a computer, a number of filing cabinets and two bookcases, one stacked with books, the other with box-files. The wall above the desk has been decorated with cut out pictures of men, in the main part naked but not explicit, with humorous captions. *If you want to sleep tonight ask him to marry you. The trouble is he only had eyes for Bob.* Bob looking in a mirror. *Little boy: Mummy when I grow up I'm going to be a man. Mummy: Don't be silly darling you can't do both*. I suppose Joseph has been in here. Sara was jealous of Amy. Did she have good cause? Amy seems as if she might know what she wants. Did that include Joseph? So what went on in this room, this cosy space? But more to the point why am I thinking like this? Am I so insanely jealous of any woman being in contact with my son that I have to paint them in any bad light I can. Straightaway I need Amy's forgiveness and I haven't even met her. If I carry on like this I will end up as disturbed as Frank. I am guilty of taking a serious and pious view of humour.

I ruffle through a few papers on her desk, without really taking much notice. I don't expect evidence of anything, reasons why my blemished son should uproot and go to France, leaving wife, daughter and career. I just want to be in the same spaces as he was when the momentous decision was made. I am pleased to have come close to Amy. I have decided to like her.

I let myself out and go directly to the office marked Dr G. Gate. I go straight in without hesitating. Much to my surprise he is sitting at his desk studying his computer screen.

"Gareth!" I utter, taken aback. "I was told you weren't available," I add quickly, as if that confers on me a moral high ground, justifies my breaking in.

He looks embarrassed and actually blushes as he says my name, Mrs Tennant. Of course, I am the parental figure in this exchange. I begin to tell him to call me Louise – he has always called me Louise before – but correct myself. Let him call me Mrs Tennant; at the moment that is what I want.

"I don't think I can help you," he says, as if I've sneaked in here in order to seduce him. The thought doesn't do me justice. This is Gareth, Joseph's good friend, a young man who has slept under my roof. In fact he's always had something of a slightly startled, perplexed look, his carefully disarranged fair hair adding to the effect, as does the curious, penetrating gaze, the rapid dark eyes and the stiff, square jaw muscles. He is handsome, with a troubled, vulnerable veneer, a match for Joseph, who was handsome in a similar, easily masculine way, but with a confident, amused outer-coating.

"But you don't know what I might ask," I say, reproving him as a parent might.

"No, of course not," he mumbles, and clicks the mouse of his computer, closing down the screen as if it were something to be kept secret. Maybe he was viewing pornography in work time and that's why he seems so shy and nervous, but I don't think so. On the other hand he could scarcely consider me an industrial spy. Whatever the cause, the screen goes blank, producing a slight acoustic ping.

"I didn't mean to interfere with your work," I say, apologizing for myself, for the foolish invasion I've created.

"No," he mumbles, waving away the need for apology, "it was nothing, I was through really."

"Why was I told you were unavailable?"

"Because, well ... I don't know. Because I can't tell you anything."

"So, you knew."

"Knew?"

"Knew that you were unavailable. You took part in that statement. I only want to talk about Joseph."

"I don't know anything."

"But you were his friend. No, no, let me say that again.

71

You are his friend. Isn't that right? Because someone dies it doesn't stop you being their friend. I'm still his mother so you must still be his friend."

Gareth shrugs, embarrassed and perturbed by my rambling, grief riven utterances, at a loss as to how to respond. I must appear a mad woman to him. And maybe I am. Surely the whole point of madness is that the victim is unaware, beyond insight, apart from occasional troubling evidence, like Munch's scream and Frank's mirror. For me it is the look on Gareth's face. It is indisputable. He has been confronted by a mad woman. He is shaken by the encounter. It will stay with him a long time, the day a dead colleague's mother cornered him in his office. But I don't care. If this is madness then there is no other way. It seems the one great insight given to the mad is to know that everyone else is insane. Why on earth would staff at Rennstadt not talk to a grieving mother unless the world was mad?

"You see, Gareth," I continue, my voice lowering, indicating confidentiality, "as his friend you can tell me so much." He is about to protest, actual anger sparking in his expression, but I go on. "I mean, you must have shared things: ideas, stories, jokes. You must know things that gave him pleasure and pain, made him frustrated and optimistic. You must have seen him excited and mad, morose and happy. I can't bear not to talk about him, act as if he didn't exist. He hasn't done anything wrong, so why is it that he is treated like a criminal? I want to talk about him all of the time, and struggle to understand why that isn't right. You see, my child grew up Gareth and moved on and spent very little time with me and stopped confiding, so his life became hidden.

"I know it's the same for all parents, all of our children

grow up and stop confiding but I'm finding it hard. You see Gareth, I don't even know what his favourite things are anymore. His favourite foods, favourite books, favourite views – landscape, political or social. Do you see my dilemma Gareth? Do you see why everything hurts so much? And yes, maybe it's all my fault. Maybe I should have kept tabs on him and known what he was becoming, known that his favourite colour remained red, but that's too hard and isn't the done thing. So I need to ask, and it's bad enough needing to ask but when people refuse to answer then it all goes crazy. Do you understand Gareth?"

He looks at me in silence, as if cowed and then quietly says: "I didn't know his favourite colour was red."

I don't know whether to laugh, cry or scream and inwardly do all three. "Yes," I say, aware of the insufficiency in my voice, its trembling and fractured nature, "red and green. It brought to mind holly and Christmas and his birthday. Holly was his favourite tree. You see, I know a lot Gareth, remember how he loved things. He loved Christmas. Well, it was his birthday as well. I've just said haven't I? He used to get sad when it was over and sometimes angry. Sad tantrums really. He wanted the pleasure to go on and on. That isn't a bad wish really, is it? We should all wish that the pleasure goes on and on."

Gareth looks at me with pity. He must feel safe, comfortable enough to allow himself to feel that, though he doesn't know what to say. But how could I expect anything else. John and I used to smile about the fact that Gareth spent his life looking down a microscope, as we saw it, because he was always tongue-tied and shy. He used to laugh a lot, edgy and loud, at the most ridiculous things. Joseph was never tongue-tied and would entertain us with stories of Gareth's mishaps – in front of Gareth – usually with girls, which Gareth always laughed at, but I wonder if he really found them as funny as he made out. It wasn't an equal friendship, but I never questioned that. I probably let Joseph down by not questioning that. Eventually Gareth manages to suggest that I sit down. I am immediately struck by the absurdity of our two positions, my standing over his desk, he protected behind it. It isn't really an equal relationship either. I smile and sit. Gareth looks pleased. I can't decipher that.

"I'm sorry Gareth," I say quietly, penitently, "I haven't asked how you are, and that wasn't right of me."

"I'm very well Mrs Tennant."

"Good, I'm pleased to hear that. And are all your family well?"

"Yes they are. In fact, I'm getting married in the summer."

"Oh, well done, good luck," I respond, which even to my ears sounds hollow and absurd, but such good luck cuts and sears me. Of course the world will carry on, a place of luck, good and ill, whether I participate or not. "Are you marrying Amy, Dr Tomlin?"

He looks decidedly shocked. "No, certainly not."

"Sorry, I don't know why I asked that. It just came to mind."

"Me and Amy, Dr Tomlin, would be the last people to be suited."

"What is she like?"

He ponders for a moment, clearly unsure what to say, and eventually opts for the single word: "Forthright." It is obvious he means strong, capable and ambitious. I like her, though can't imagine what she would make of me.

"Is she here?"

"No, she really is in London."

"I think I would have liked to talk to her." Gareth looks uneasy. "You don't seem too sure about that Gareth. Would I not like to talk with Amy?"

"I don't know. I can't say, can I?"

"You seemed to be suggesting something."

"Amy was quite sore at Joseph."

"Sore?"

"I think she's still sore at Joseph."

Sore. It seems such a strange word for Gareth to utter. There is something quaint and yet powerful about it. I suppose there is something quaint and yet powerful about Gareth. He is at once young and otherworldly, a scientist and man, theoretical and marriageable. I should be pleased for him. Despite not wanting to see me, his is a pleasant nature. I like to think that Joseph was fond of him. I can't bear to think that their friendship really wasn't equal, or worse, wasn't a friendship at all. I want Joseph to have had friendships, not just alliances and fellow-travellers. Friendship demands human qualities. It might not be useful, but I can't believe that Joseph would only have had a mind for people being useful, which I suppose is what I suspected Sara of doing. Everything seemed so calculated, their identity contrived. Identity should be accidental, maybe even accident-prone. Gareth strikes me as accident-prone. And I didn't think Joseph was. You see, Gareth, I know so little; nothing in fact.

"Were you good friends Gareth, you and Joseph? You always seemed like good friends. You giggled like good friends."

He looks me right in the eye, letting me know he is not

embarrassed by the question. "He would have been my best man. I was his best man."

"I remember your speech, funny and touching, antics."

"I miss him."

"Sore?"

"Yes, I'm sore. I don't mind admitting it. We talked about everything, work things naturally, but other things as well, real things. I miss that, the chats we had."

He falls silent and shrugs, unable to say more, remembering, I suppose, a style of conversation rather than particular ones, because that's how memory is, fragments and hints that one tries to piece together, a knitting and matching that refuses to cohere and keeps falling apart. Yes, Gareth, I too miss the chats we had. He was good. His voice glowed with enthusiasm and confidence. The things he had seen, the things he understood, the strange world revealed to him, scientist and son.

"He was good at making connections," I say, trying to summons his chats.

"Yes he was," Gareth concurs. "That's why he was so good at research. He'd remember a paper, often on something completely different, and fit it with what he was doing and come up with something startling and new. And he'd have the right questions to ask, just instinctively know what needed more thought."

"Why is Amy sore?"

"Because he walked out on their research and it's never been finished."

I frown at him. The Amy I have constructed would never be that petulant. Sore seems so much stronger than disappointment over a work project. But of course the word is Gareth's. Gareth is sore. He has lost a best man. Having a best man is quite a boast. I can feel for his soreness. His loss consoles me, slightly. I will have to recreate Amy, remove the irony from her collection of posters and replace it with something else, possibly chagrin.

Gareth smiles vaguely and says: "She's sore that he isn't here. She liked him here. She liked him."

"Were they having an affair?"

"No, no, I don't think so."

"And she is forthright."

"Confident," Gareth says, as if correcting an earlier opinion.

"In a bad way?"

He shrugs. "I don't know." He smiles at me, comfortable with me at last, possibly entertained by me, pleased with my ways.

"Why did he leave?"

He immediately looks troubled again. "I can't say Mrs Tennant."

Troubled and formal. "But you had chats. You spoke of things. He would have said something to you."

"I don't mean that. It's just . . . I don't know."

"You mean you're not allowed to say. That's what you've been trying to tell me, and I didn't get it. You're not allowed to say."

"It's just company policy."

"Why?"

"There's a lot of secrecy in drug companies. There has to be. There's a lot of money involved, so research is well guarded."

"Who told you that you can't talk to me?"

"You need to talk to Mr Davidson."

"But I'm talking to you."

"I can't say."

"Are you frightened?"

"No, of course not. It's just rules, company regulation."

"But surely you can talk to a friend's mother."

"No, I really can't."

"Well, talk to a friend. You've stayed in my house. We've been friends."

"Look Mrs Tennant, all I can say is that he was unhappy when some research was withdrawn."

"What research?"

"I don't know. Look, it happens all of the time. Some things get the money, some things get chopped. I really don't know why Joseph was so bothered."

"Do you think Amy will talk to me?"

"There's nothing to say, Mrs Tennant."

"But there must be, Gareth or why spend so much time not saying it?"

"I really must get back to my work."

"You want me to leave?"

"But you have to go. You can't stay here all day."

"I'm sorry Gareth. It's all become a little deranged, but I'm sure you understand something of what the feeling is. The more I ask the less I know and I suspect it's because I'm not listening properly. Do you know, Gareth, that whenever I think of Joseph, which is all of the time, a piece of music goes over and over in my head, *Spiegel im Spiegel*. Now why do you think that is?"

"Because he liked it?"

"Yes." I hadn't really expected an answer, my question entirely rhetorical. "He did in fact, liked it very much. But I don't think that's the whole answer. There's something else, a reason that I should hear that particular music. Maybe I'm lucky. It is a beautiful piece of music. If it was something else it might send me crazy, but it doesn't do that, or does it? How can I say, Gareth?"

"I don't know what to say, Mrs Tennant."

"Tell me the truth Gareth."

He looks horrified. At that moment the door behind me opens. A shiver runs through me. There is alarm in Gareth's face, which he can't disguise, though he is trying to look relaxed. I turn around to face whoever has entered. There is a security guard standing in the doorway. He is middle-aged, with a heavy round face, with staring, distrustful eyes, though maybe I'm imposing that on him, knowing his role, knowing that I am to be ejected. He has my coat in his hand, holding it as one might a rag for a sniffer-dog.

"Mrs Tennant was just leaving. She wanted to know if her son had left any of his effects here, which he has not," Gareth says without conviction.

I stand up and smile at Gareth. I am well aware that he is telling the security guard who I am. The name must have significance, be familiar to the entire staff. I find that surprising, bewildering. Each event deepens my incomprehension. "Thank you Dr Gate," I say, "it was very kind of you to listen. I hope all goes well with you for the wedding. Do you have any thoughts about the music?"

"I should keep listening I think."

"Yes, I agree. Goodbye Dr Gate."

The security guard moves aside allowing me past and holds out my coat for me to take. He is not about to put it over my shoulders for me. He doesn't handle me but as we make our way to the lift I feel like a criminal being taken into custody. It is belittling. A series of images rush through my mind: school day punishments from irate, disturbed nuns; cowering in a corner as my father swears and strikes my mother; sitting in the back of a police car, guilty until reprieved. There is a child in me that suffers them all, the accumulated years of punishment, unjust and just. The guard doesn't speak but acts as if I have disappointed him, affronted him in some way. As the lift doors open I say: "I am upset about my son, that's all." I realize that I'm trying to summon up my grief to confer on me some dignity. He doesn't answer. To my surprise he follows me into the lift. Evidently I am to be escorted right off the premises. The ground floor receptionist eyes me coolly as I am led through the lobby. I may have got her into trouble so it is understandable. But what do they fear from me? Is a grieving mother bad for business? Nothing makes sense. On the steps the guard finally speaks. "Goodbye, Mrs Tennant." It is final. I am never to return. A part of my son's life is off-limits to me.

I ring for my ally, pleased to discover that he has indeed waited. He wants to know whether my trip was satisfactory. I tell him that it's hard to gauge. He says he'll give it another few years then call it a day, there's no fun in it anymore, though he does meet nice people from time to time, which from the look on his face in the mirror includes me. No, I think, there is no fun. My trip has been a disaster. I want to run back to London as quickly as I can, back to my own way of thinking, my own version of things, back to my own perverse normality.

Chapter Six

The southern offices of Rennstadt are grander than their northern branch. They stand back from a road in Esher, fronted by a mighty billboard. The surrounding landscape has no focus or symmetry. The roads are numerous, busy and fast, with endless roundabouts, passing sports fields, small parks and random buildings. Most things are built away from the road, shaded by trees and walls. The road merely connects. The aesthetic is small scale and close up, the larger picture arbitrary and functional. Development has been cellular. I feel adrift. Without a taxi I would be lost, a ridiculous pedestrian. It seems I increasingly need guides to get me to the places I need to be. In function if not appearance I am letting myself grow old. Age is deliberate. I want to be out of step and I want to be seen to be out of step. My floundering is not coquettish, a trick to attract attention and assistance, but a judgement, a moment of dissent. I refuse the mechanism of this world: it took my son.

Maybe, once upon a time, I should have considered architecture. I seem to have become a commentator of the modern landscape, a critic even. The idea is absurd of course. I could never have stood the rigours of the essential science or the demand of costs. My materials, my made up objects, are small scale, intimate. I'm always thinking I should have done this or that, ridiculous things like become an anthropologist or archaeologist – and now architect – and that's just the a's, but it's all nonsense. I love my little constructions, minor additions in the sum of creation but mine all the same. My little works were behind my fall-out with Frank. I have always wanted to be useful, to give pleasure: he wanted art to resist inter-pretation. But what's the point? He was arrogant, stupid and deluded. I ran away, ran to John.

The taxi driver hasn't spoken at any time, except to utter things under his breath, particularly when the office sounds on his radio, a fairly constant stream of pickups and destinations. He isn't relaxed driving but at war with everything: other drivers, other cars and his own gear-stick and steering wheel. He directs the car with great movements of his shoulders and only brakes at the last moment, leaving scarcely any space between his car and the one in front. I don't know how he faces each day with such impatience and temper.

After a while, I realize that he doesn't hate it but loves it. This is his game. He is a man of action, his mission to navigate through the dense absurdity of contemporary development. Is it a good mission? Does it rank as an example of man's basically tragic state? Perhaps. Who am I to say otherwise? In the end it will kill him, stroke or heart-attack; he's way overweight. He probably gets little exercise and eats on the move. I'm not surprised he hasn't spoken to me. He probably despises anyone who can afford his services, especially someone asking for a destination like Rennstadt, with its ostentatious billboard, fish-pond with golden carp and revolving door. I am becoming so judgemental. I have lost my love. I simply exist. He is impatient when I ask for his number. He doesn't have a card so writes it quickly on a scrap of paper. I have to check the number with him. He drives off at speed. Thank God it's the office number and not his so the return driver may be different. I enjoyed thinking the taxi driver in Leeds was an ally, though it doesn't surprise me that here they aren't. There isn't enough time or space for alliances; it isn't cost-effective.

The entrance to Rennstadt is very grand. It is a gallery of abstract paintings – originals not prints – pot-plants and desks. The desks are arranged in a broken semicircle with shining polished steps between and ramps running from both right and left towards lifts to the rear. A security guard saunters around, exchanging a word and a smile with the girls at the desks intent on their computer screens. If I'd needed to break in here it would have been a wholly more daring affair, demanding real criminal acumen. Luckily I have an appointment. Mr Davidson's secretary had no hesitation in putting my name in his diary, and didn't even inquire what the meeting was about. It seemed to me that I was expected to call, but that is absurd, unless the Leeds' office made contact, warning them, but I don't see how I could be that important.

The girl at the desk, who is oriental with long, straight, jet-black hair, is extremely polite and has an exquisite smile. I feel heartened. I am being treated to courtesy. Word has not spread to this desk that I am an obsessive, a grieving trouble-maker. She tells me that I am expected and to go right up, the fourth floor, and directs me to the lift. On the fourth floor I am greeted by Miss Steele – Mr Davidson's PA, she informs me – who is smartly dressed in grey jacket and skirt, and a white blouse cut low enough to reveal the outline of her substantial breasts. Offering no more than that introduction she walks briskly away and I assume I am to follow. She leads me into a spacious office, announces me and leaves. Mr Davidson gets up from his desk, smiling, and offers his hand. He doesn't shake my hand but holds it, holds it for longer than might be deemed normal, but I can tell by his expression that he isn't treating this as normal but rather assumes he will have to console me. He takes his jacket from the back of his chair and puts it on. I am to be afforded formality. He is a tall man, probably in his late thirties, with dark hair swept back from his head, revealing a dominant forehead below which his face is sharp and triangular. He smiles and gestures for me to sit and resumes his own.

"I am very sorry for your loss, Mrs Tennant," he begins immediately, his voice slightly husky, catching in his throat. "We all are. Joseph was very popular."

"Yes," I say, not particularly agreeing with anything, simply uncertain with a stranger's sympathy, unsure what I am supposed to do with it.

He smiles again, the gesture somewhat awkward. He is not easy with me – who is in the face of drastic loss, someone symbolizing all and everyone's fragility and mortality? I expected him to be older. Perhaps an older man would have succumbed to my symbolism rather more. I expected a plain looking, rather aloof, staid business-man, not a good-looking young man. He makes me feel older than I am. I can't work that out, other than with the dismal thought that I know I am probably not attractive to him. I flatter myself with the word probably. Mr Davidson waits. He has worked out how to make it easier for himself. I have come to him. It is my place to speak. He is happy waiting.

"I just thought," I begin falteringly, "that it might be helpful to talk to you."

He smiles again, leaning forward, his elbows on his desk, his fingers spread across his chin. "I don't know that I will be of any help, but if I can, then of course."

"It's just . . . well, I thought my son was working for you, in France I mean."

"Me personally, do you mean?"

"No, no, the company. I thought he had gone with his work."

Mr Davidson splays his fingers, two spindly blossoms either side of his cheeks, indicating sympathy for my lack of understanding, but also a comical assertion that that's how it was. I want him to say something but he continues to wait.

"It was a bit of a shock, that's all."

I eye him intently, pleading to be afforded some understanding, some inkling as to why Joseph would abandon the life he had. When I said, that's all, it was absurd. It is just a starting point. After the shock there are a million and one considerations. They contend, bringing to mind contradictory and sometimes crazy narratives. My son abandoned his wife and child because . . . (the mother wanting to preserve her child's prestige imagines, tells herself) because he was still with the company and it was all a monumental misunderstanding. Or the mother tells herself that her son fell fatally in love with someone else, but had every intention of remitting money to wife and child. He must have been working for someone, needed references, some contact.

He sits back, his hands in front of him in an attitude of prayer. "Of course," he says, "it was a shock to all of us. No one ever expects, but . . . but I wouldn't suggest that I could know how you feel."

"No," I respond gratefully, thankful that he hasn't suggested that he knows how I feel. Even I don't really know that. Of course he may have experienced many things; he

85

certainly speaks with an air of maturity. "I'm pleased you could see me all the same."

"Of course, the least I could do, though I must admit that I don't quite know why you wanted to see me."

"Do I need a reason?" I snap, surprising myself with my own petulance. He doesn't respond. He purses his lips, apparently suffused with compassion. I feel my temper physically possessing me, my mind trying to transform it into ideas and words, though at the same time acknowledging its irrationality. But why shouldn't I want to see someone my son worked with, worked for? Is it so strange? My son died in mysterious circumstances and I have a need to contend with that mystery. People he worked with have been told not to speak to me. I utter that spontaneously. "Employees have been instructed not to talk to me."

He shakes his head and smiles, indulgently, parental. "No, Mrs Tennant, that is not the case. We would never make such an instruction."

"Gareth, Dr Gate, was told not to speak to me."

"Again Mrs Tennant I can assure you that is not the case. There may be things Dr Gate would rather he didn't say to you. I can fully appreciate that. I find Dr Gate rather reserved. I respect it."

"I'm sorry?" I say, questioning the meaning of what he has just said. He looks uncomprehending. "Do you mean I don't, or didn't, respect Dr Gate?"

"There are protocols and procedures about discussing company matters. Dr Gate quite rightly felt obliged to follow those principles."

"I just wondered what my son's favourite books were." Mr Davidson smiles, but breaks eye contact. "I wondered if he knew his favourite view."

86

"I'm sure as his mother you would be best positioned to answer those things."

"Yes, you would think so."

"Or his wife. Joseph was married."

"Yes, I know."

"I wasn't suggesting that you didn't know that, Mrs Tennant."

"No, I mean you are right. A wife is the person who should know all these things, but I thought there would be no harm in asking Dr Gate, Gareth. They were friends. Gareth has stayed at our house, our being Joseph's father and me."

"These are personal matters Mrs Tennant. I don't quite know what to say."

"Why was Joseph in France?"

He shakes his head, and extends his hands expressing incomprehension.

"He wasn't working for you?"

"No Mrs Tennant, Joseph was no longer working for us. I really am not in any position to tell you anything about Joseph being in France. I can't really advise who you should talk to other than his wife. Do you get on, you and your daughter-in-law, I mean, if you don't find the question impertinent?"

"As daughter-in-law and mother tend to do."

"Mine get on very well. I'm lucky I guess."

"You are married then?"

"Yes Mrs Tennant, I am married."

"Good luck with that."

"I've been married for twelve years, Mrs Tennant, and have two young children."

"Thank you. I feel I know you very well now. Dr Gate says Joseph wasn't happy when you withdrew some research he was working on."

"Did he?"

"Have I got Gareth into trouble, breaking company protocol and policy?"

"Of course not, Mrs Tennant. As with any organization, funding is tight, and some projects prosper and others have to be sidelined. That's the way in this business. It's unfortunate sometimes, but we can't put resources into everything we would like to. I didn't know that Joseph had concerns. He certainly didn't talk to me about them."

"Would he have spoken to Amy?"

"Dr Tomlin. No, I don't suppose so."

"You seem sure."

"I know the people I work with, Mrs Tennant. We work closely."

"Am I able to speak to Amy?"

"Of course you could, but unfortunately she is in Madrid at present."

"Holiday?"

He smiles, indulging me again. It is evidently an absurd suggestion. "She's speaking at a conference. She is quite an asset, a rising star. But you didn't come here to listen to me praise one of our employees."

"I don't mind."

He smiles again and takes a quick look at his watch. "I would like to be able to say something you'd want to hear Mrs Tennant, but I don't know anything about Joseph's life after he left us."

"Is that why he resigned, because his research wasn't funded? He always was a bit, well, stubborn, bloody-minded at times. I know that."

"Look Mrs Tennant, this is delicate."

"Protocol and policy."

"No, just difficult," he says rather sharply, his expression contracting with a moment of temper. "I don't find this easy."

"I'm sorry for that, but I don't find it easy either."

"I appreciate that Mrs Tennant. I think we should just leave things as they are."

I seize on that. It suggests an understanding from which I am being excluded, but can't comprehend why. My son obviously battled here and I want to know about it. "No, Mr Davidson, I don't want to leave things as they are. I'd like to know why my son left this company and I think I have a right to know."

"He was sacked."

"Sorry?" I utter, feeling as if I have been struck. I simply gaze ahead, avoiding Mr Davidson's eyes, despising the control he has, his knowledge.

"His contract was terminated."

"Can I know why?"

"Of course, though I'd rather not tell you."

"I need to know everything Mr Davidson. I can't carry on with mystery."

"I'm afraid that Joseph's own personal drug use was getting out of hand."

"My son never touched drugs. I am afraid of drugs Mr Davidson, really rather in dread of them, and that is how I taught him."

Mr Davidson shrugs, his expression quizzing yet compassionate. "I've seen it before Mrs Tennant. People in this business think they can manage it. I've seen bright, serious young men who think their knowledge makes them immune, not just young men either. We have to stay on the right side of the fence. The whisper in this business is *self-medicating*, as if calling it that makes it all right

89

and safe. But it isn't. And I am afraid it isn't tolerated. I'm sorry Mrs Tennant."

"I don't believe you."

"I wouldn't expect you to, as his mother, but it doesn't make it untrue."

"You can't know the conversations we had, the things he said."

"It is tragic Mrs Tennant, tragic that such talent is wasted."

"It isn't true."

"I didn't ask you to come here, Mrs Tennant. You insisted on knowing. Remember that."

"I know my son, Mr Davidson, and I know that what you say can't be true."

I sound melodramatic, a woman playing a mother's part. But what is left to me but to resist, stamp my foot and say it isn't true. I can't have known him so little, been so clouded and befuddled by love that I couldn't see the grown-up he was. I am a mother, not an imbecile. I would have known, seen clues, picked up hints and give-aways. Every parent knows something of their child's failings. Mine was slightly arrogant, over confident, didn't take criticism without retaliation, didn't always know when teasing passed over into insults. For the rest he was good, a model human being, tender-hearted, and despite the trivia of his sometimes shallow world motivated by decent thought. They cannot and will not take that child away from me. He cannot have been a lie, a made up sham. I will not accept it. I still have a responsibility.

Mr Davidson is eyeing me, his attention sympathetic and annoyed, both I'd say in equal measure. He obviously feels that my protectiveness, as he reads it, is misplaced. He wants me to accept that my child moved on and became the man he insists he knows. I have to draw a line.

"I'm sorry, Mr Davidson, I know you think I am blind to who my son is, but I'm not. I just know there's something not right about this. My son would never abuse drugs and he would never leave his wife and child."

"I'm sorry, Mrs Tennant. None of this is easy."

"I can't leave it like this."

"I really am sorry, Mrs Tennant."

"I know you are a busy man."

"Yes, I am in fact."

"Don't worry I can find my own way out."

"Mrs Tennant," he calls when I reach the door, "believe me, I wish it were otherwise."

"Thank you for your time, Mr Davidson, I know more than I did."

"Goodbye Mrs Tennant."

I know that all this is a lie.

Chapter Seven

I close the house door, having achieved sanctuary, and stand with my back to it as if resisting intruders, my mind reeling, turning over and over in its own indeterminable space. I can't remember much about the journey home. It comes to me as a sequence of scenes.

On leaving Rennstadt I found myself on a dual carriageway. I obviously shouldn't have been there as there was no proper walkway just the grass verge. The grass was wet around my ankles, the morning having been cold, at the edge of the city probably frosty. Some cars hooted. Were they mocking me, appreciating me or trying to frighten me? It was fear they provoked. And fear built up. It took over my thinking, disordered and exposed me. I felt I should run. At one point I did. I ran along the grass verge, the traffic rushing past me, large lorries creating sudden shade and cold. I found myself at a roundabout and really didn't know how to negotiate it. I must have seemed like an escaped mad woman as I demanded directions to the station of a man with a Labrador. I told myself that there was something safe about a man with such a dog. I can't remember his answer, but I must have registered it because I managed to end up on a train, managed to return to known places.

There was confusion at the junction of Leighton Road, traffic snarled up back on Fortess Road. Of course it always is. Every day is the same. But a van driver mounted the pavement in front of the Assembly Rooms pub and went around a number of stalled cars, bullied another car to go into the side then sped away along Highgate Road, sounding his horn a number of times as he did. And then it was all over, and the former confusion went on as if nothing had happened. So much about living in London is like that, about simply coping with it. People feel successful just because they can cope. I rushed away, certain that I was not coping. The ways I have learnt no longer work. I need a different knowledge altogether. At that moment I sought seclusion.

Lady Margaret Road with its Georgian doorways, columns and arches, its stained glass windows and yellow brick walls, is a haven. I love its peace, its relative quiet and its domesticity. I love the thought of its humanity, its myriad lives taking place with only narrow walls between. I love crowded London, its cluttered spaces, its out of sight proximity. I feel safer in its mass than out of it.

The image of myself running alongside an unknown dual carriageway fills me with dread. My son died on the road, his body run over three times. I hear the slamming of breaks, a scream, the sound of impact. Lives are taken, in haste, pitilessly. I see myself the driver, face agape. I hear notes of music. I can't make sense of that. I must be going mad.

I understand that people often feel they are going mad when they are in pain. My counsellor tells me it's extremely common. He regularly reminds me, with a great flourish of emphasis: You have to remember though, that you are not going mad. I look at him coyly, my girlish habits not easily ditched, and smile. Would going mad not be easier to deal with than incessant grief? How much can my body and mind stand? I am being shredded, left in pieces. I can't be expected to emerge unscathed. And yet madness is portrayed as the worst of all solutions. Madness is not to be permitted. Everything I experience is normal. Well, if that is the case, is it normal to feel that I have been followed? I'm sure that a car came out of Rennstadt and patrolled the dual carriageway while I made my fitful, amateurish escape. And then again on the train, I'm sure there was someone watching me, at times openly, his eyes straight on me. If I tell my counsellor will he say that these are perfectly normal manifestations of the grieving process? Process! To hell with process! I don't believe in it. I don't believe in healing. I believe in chaos and break up. I believe in hostile fate. Whoever said the world had to make sense? It doesn't, doesn't add up at all.

Joseph used to try and convince me otherwise, determined to take in hand his artist, sceptical, all over the place mother. He described the ability of mathematics to glimpse new worlds, trying to find a language I might comprehend, one that my closed mind wouldn't dismiss. He said: If you draw a circle – catching my attention immediately – and surround it with equally sized circles so that they all touch the number is always six. If you keep expanding you can work out mathematically how many circles there will be with each increase. Turn the circles into spheres, two dimensions into three, and the maths can still predict the necessary number. But when image stops, say at four, five or ten dimensions, the maths can still continue where the eye can't. Maths can reveal hidden dimensions, new worlds, a new concept of space time, completely new versions of reality.

He laughed all the time he tried to explain such things to me, attempting to take me to visionary worlds where the eye couldn't penetrate but theory could, casting me in the role of naïve disbeliever, delightful but ill-informed. He loved those games we played, the two of us trying to outdo each other – my retaliation being that art can reveal how all space is produced, created as much by looking as being – the artist and the scientist jousting, playful and friends. My son was my friend. We had managed that compact. We understood nothing of what the other said but understood each other impeccably. I know my son. He would do no harm. I am being told a lie and I don't know why. And now I am being followed. Of course, it is possible that I am going mad and nothing is real, neither what the eye sees nor the mind reveals, all of it a trick, a con, played out for someone else's fun. With a thought like that I really must be losing my marbles. I am becoming a match for Frank in his most drug-induced states. My counsellor is right, that would never do.

I move away from the door, throw down my jacket and pour myself a drink, despite the fact that it is still early and way before even my time, then work my way through the house, looking down into the street from each window that allows it. I insist to myself that I don't expect to see anyone looking back but can't stop myself from doing it. Besides, if surveillance really were taking place I imagine it would be more sophisticated than seeing someone lurking about on Lady Margaret Road. I think to call John. I need him, need him so much. I am being followed, which I admit must be very unlikely, and don't know what to do. I need help. I need to be taken in hand. Perhaps I should call my counsellor.

At the same moment as I think that the telephone rings. The sound startles me. It seems an alien sound, as if it hasn't rung for such a long time, which is absurd: of course the telephone rings, rings all of the time, John calls, Vivien calls, Vivien acting out the part of Vivien, sister and rescuer, cold calls, salesmen and crooks, though not colleagues or friends, not really, perhaps someone from the support group. But at this moment it sounds as if from a different time altogether, a much older time. Eventually I rush and pick up the receiver and hesitantly say hello.

"Yes, hello," a woman's voice responds. I don't recognize the voice. It is hushed and slow. After the introductory two words there is silence. I find it disconcerting.

"Who is it?" I ask. "Who is it you want?"

"Mrs Tennant?"

"Yes, it's Mrs Tennant. Can I help?"

"No, well, no . . . I don't mean that."

"Sorry, what is it you want?"

"There is someone you should speak to."

"Sorry?"

"Dominique Dufour, she'll talk to you."

"What do you mean?"

"I can give you a number. She's in Paris. Ring her."

"Who is this?"

"You'll need to write the number down, but keep it safe. Maybe don't put her name with it."

"I need you to explain."

"Are you ready?"

"Is that Amy?" There is no reply. "Is it, Dr Tomlin?"

"Do you want the number or not?"

"Yes, I want the number."

Without waiting she gives me it, pronouncing the digits in pairs: "01 47 07 77 77. Just ask for her. If she's there, she'll talk to you."

"Dominique Dufour," I repeat quietly, wanting confirmation that I've got it right, got the whole conversation right, the strangeness of it, perhaps confirming that I've accepted it for what it seems.

"This isn't Amy. I don't know anybody called Amy," she replies and hangs up.

I hold the phone at my ear for a while, wanting the conversation to continue, wanting to verify the substance of it, until the phone alarms. I check the number that called but it was withheld. I can only guess. I sit down, shaken and disturbed. The terrible reality is that there is something mysterious about Joseph's dying. I have been advised to talk to someone in Paris. The advice suggests that there is something to hear. A shiver runs through my body. I am being drawn into something very real that seems entirely without reality. I don't know what to make of it. I go to a window and look out. It is turning dark and there are people making their way home. I don't trust them, not one of them. What is happening to me?

Chapter Eight

It is bitterly cold in Paris, with occasional snow flurries. I am staying in a grubby hotel in Rue de la Roche Foucauld, between Pigalle and Trinité. The street seems to connect two distinct worlds, one of sex shops and sleaze and the other of chocolate and pastry shops. In all honesty I vacillate between the two. I have a tourist's eye for trade of all kinds. In the night time, returning from dinner and the wine of numerous cafés I turn into a positive voyeur. The discreet character of the street becomes explicit. During the day it is the pharmacy and the small grocers that stand out, in the night the girls. They sit in the windows outlined by fluorescent lights, blue, red or orange, live goods. The Blue Cat I find particularly alluring, its blueness the blueness of stained glass, deep and meditative. Paris creates juxtaposition, its cultures rubbing shoulders. On my second night one of the girls from The Blue Cat waved. The gesture seemed devoid entirely of sarcasm, though I don't know. I waved back and then we went about our business, mine to return to the hotel, hers to whatever a shop-window girl does. She had stately thighs, milky and rounded like a lunar surface beneath cold space.

I don't know what John made of my garbled explanation that I was going to France. He seemed angry, which I couldn't understand.

"That's ridiculous," he said, quietly, but with impatience.

"Any more ridiculous than being in America?" I asked, not accusing him, wondering.

He was quiet for a while and then firmly stated: "I am working. I have a contract. I have to work. It's what I do."

"Yes," I agreed, "it's textbook stuff, you should work. I just have to go to Paris."

"But why? Why now? Why Paris?"

"We used to love Paris," I said.

"We still do, don't we?"

"No, I don't think we do, we lost the habit."

"Don't go," he insisted.

I thought for a while before responding, hearing the command in his voice. I shook my head and simply uttered: "I have to."

"No, no you don't, you're making it so much harder for yourself, for us."

Again I said nothing. For some reason I didn't tell him what Sara had said, what Mr Davidson had said, about being followed, or that Dominique Dufour would talk to me. I don't know why I left John out of that. I don't know if I was protecting Joseph or him, or perhaps myself. It was too difficult to understand. Eventually I whispered: "No, John, I'm not making it harder. It will be easier, I promise."

I told him that I loved him. I meant it. He angrily replied that he loved me. It was heart breaking to be on different continents, so far apart, to have so many secrets that I didn't understand.

For days I have been a tourist, taking in the usual sites, the obvious ones for me: Musée du Louvre, Musée D'Orsay and Musée Marmottan, the artist paying homage, revisiting scenes of former passions, where I invested love in canvas, in two dimensional realities. Grief nullifies such passion, though, and takes significance away. I have berated myself so many times, telling myself that I am here for Joseph, not on a sightseeing tour. But I can't do it, not immediately. I need to orientate myself, learn confidence in the language again. I'm sure my counsellor would applaud and tell me it is right to spend time on cherished things. The trouble is it all wearies me. I weary me. Trying to remember the enthusiasm with which I celebrated twentieth century art wearies me. I seem a sham. It didn't prepare me for human trial. And yet love has not turned entirely sour. Love just seems insubstantial, the object world insufficient.

By night I drink and watch the night slip by, watch it in the eyes of the other watchers, and that is restorative. There is life in that. It is so cold that everyone is wrapped up, covered in grey layers. I have never known Paris to be so grey. It seems quite spiritless. A newspaper hoarding says there have been riots in the suburbs. I feel the tension of that. Maybe I am conscious of being a woman alone. The people on the metro seem wary and distrustful. Is it real – the riots must be real – or is it all down to me? Maybe I am making Paris up as I go along, drawing it in my own drab image. On the first night I was here I walked up from Pigalle toward Montmartre but couldn't find a restaurant that was open. It was like a winter ghost town. Eventually I found one. The waiter spoke the most perfect, idiomatic English. He was quite self-effacing about it. His girlfriend was Australian, he explained, so he had picked bits up. I was pleased. I was weary of trying to speak French.

Je me débrouille en Francais – I get by in French. I have said that so many times already, to waiters, ticket-collectors, anyone generous enough to comment on the fact that I am speaking French. They invariably say my French is excellent, but I know that is flirting. (The flirtation is not without certain pleasures. I am so shallow, so needy.) John speaks very well, particular about tenses and the correct prepositions, even mastering the subjunctive. I want simply to be understood. I have perhaps set my ambitions too low. I have that usual shambling whisper of the English trying to speak a foreign language, the general lack of confidence forcing me to take any short-cut I can. I get flustered whereas I should enjoy my ability. I used to speak well, once upon a time, and wonder where it has gone. Maybe I am losing skills, losing words the way John's father lost words, drip by drip, the brain becoming atrophied. What other deficits am I developing?

I try to imagine a world without language, and wonder how much would cease to exist? Abstract nouns would have no basis whatsoever. So, what of love, faith and grief – and the greatest of these is? Yes, what would we make of love in a world without words, in our cognitively privileged world? How to express the message? But, what message? There would be no message in a world without words. There would be no notion of love at all. My wordless son would never say: I am sacred, comfot me. (Is that the dyslexia of the hardened drug-user?) What worlds we have constructed with our words – world of laughter, world of shame, world of hope, world of waste, world of wait and see.

When Joseph was here he would send funny, entertaining emails about his ridiculous inadequacies with the language and how he regretted his lame attempts at school. He reminded me that I was always pestering him to persevere with French, pointing out to him how useful it would be to be able to say, a slice of, a little bit more of or less of, this, that and the other. And guess what, he wrote, mother was absolutely right. (Surely, a little bit more, said to a drug-dealer, couldn't be the phrase which highlighted his shortcomings, could it? And, surely I do not have doubts about that?) He said he ended up saying things because he could. In one conversation he was trying to say that he made experiments, meaning chains of chemicals, molecules, compounds, and worded it as: *Je fais les jouets*. I make toys, playthings. I could hear his laughter in the message. Jouet was a word he remembered. It came out. The woman he was talking to was thrilled and thought he was a toymaker. She even took him home and showed him her collection of dolls. He never said what happened after that.

Of course he made the usual English error of saying he was pretty when he meant he was happy: *Je suis joli*. The truth is that he was both – a pretty, happy toymaker; pretty and happy and hopeless with language. I am sacred, comfot me. I need to do what I came here for. I need focus. *J'ai besoin de* . . . I have need of so much.

The hotel is cold. My room is bare and dismal. There are watermarks across the wall. The furniture, a wardrobe and dressing-table, are old and chipped, made of dark wood. The shower and toilet are tucked in a corner close to the head of the bed with an extremely narrow doorway. The carpet beside the bed is mildly damp. The shower drips continuously. There are yellow stains all over the cubicle.

There is a small safe inside the wardrobe. There were no instructions with it so I had to go back to the reception after I'd checked in and ask for an explanation. Later a man came to my room to take me through it. In fact he wasn't very sure. It was something of an accident that between us we worked out how to set a combination. I joked that I wasn't a rich woman, but nevertheless . . . , to which he smiled appreciatively. John always said that making a joke in a foreign language was proof of skill.

It is my fourth morning here. Today I am going to stop being a tourist. I rang the British Consul yesterday. This morning I have an appointment. We are to discuss the police report. I have scarcely slept, despite a liberal quantity of wine. I am cold and nervous. I view the shower with dread. It is so small it is impossible to avoid touching surfaces, surfaces which are cold and wet. There is a radiator in the room but it is insufficient. The bed is high off the floor and covered in sheets, blankets and covers which are uncomfortably heavy. I hate weight on me when I'm trying to sleep, but it is too cold to have any skin exposed. I need to get on, stop thinking of minor discomfort and inconvenience. Today I have an appointment in a foreign city.

Chapter Nine

Over breakfast of black coffee and croissants the tune plays over in my mind, slow and resonant. There is so much beauty in it. Is that the mind playing tricks, creating consolation where in reality there is none? The mind is provocative and protective, only allowing access to those things that shouldn't destroy it. But in this case beauty and barbarity coincide with each note. There is something about this tune which I can't work out, but it exists. This tune has become that of a dead boy, my dead boy, a beautiful boy meeting a terrible death. Already I am making up stories, pre-empting the police report. Of course I am. There are stories within stories, and I scurry about inside mine like a rat along miles of sewerage, no longer sure of the purpose of anything, ignorant entirely of whether I am looking for escape or discovery. I have to trust in events.

This morning I awoke cold, drenched in sweat, my whole body frozen in its own juice. I had been dreaming that I was caught in a vast Gothic hotel resplendent with plush reception and great chandeliered dining room but with a maze of stairways and corridors hidden behind the façade. I was confined to those, escaping something or someone, certain that my crime was on the verge of discovery. The stairs twisted this way and that, spiralling into depths like the stairways of old castles. At each turn there was the possibility of disclosure. And then, coming through one room, dashing from one stairway to another, I was assaulted by a group of children, or maybe they were midgets, or maybe yet again made up fairy tale creatures, part human part monkey. But they kept coming at me, biting, wanting to dismember me, do violence to my body. I fought them off but they kept coming, and I found I had to keep spinning round because they were sneaking behind me, and that made my blood run cold. The thought that they were behind me filled me with dread. So I spun and I fought, and then I realized the only way to escape was to kill them, because if I didn't kill them they'd simply keep coming until I was in shreds.

Then, because the dream had summoned them, there were knives. I had one in each hand, but so did they and there was a sequence of cuttings and slashes. At that point I awoke, frozen, helpless, craving, lost in this dingy room.

I lay there in my own sweat for some time, half-awake, still half-asleep, in transit between two terrible hotels. And then there was a moment of greater lucidity, one where I realized that I might have died at the hands of the assassins, whoever they were, and I began to wonder what my final dream on earth might be. Of course, there are any number of final things, the last word, smile, song, but dreams are beyond one's control. Besides, dreams in all likelihood will be the last thing of all. Would it be a dream of heaven, dream of hell, dream of a hermit's cell? And for a moment I felt an intense, heartrending fear. When I finally fully awoke, I felt relieved and pleased to be in my awful room. To wonder about the ultimate dream was not without satisfaction.

John has terrible dreams. More often than not he won't talk about them, but it's obvious he has trouble shaking them off, finding the divide between dream and reality.

Sometimes he develops deep black rings around his eyes, despite the fact that he's slept, such is the force of them. Maybe it is part of the cost of his reasonableness and the comfort he gives. Usually he looks at the world conducting itself around him with ruthless, intellectual vigour, but then sometimes with bafflement. The bafflement is strange, it is so needy and childlike, even childish. His dreams leave him washed out and wasted. They always come to him as detailed stories with fully formed characters, aping thrillers and crime stories, barbaric and pitiless. I don't know how long he can endure such dreams, surely not a lifetime anyway.

I can't help but look at the people around the breakfast room and judge them by whether I think they dream or not. It is an arrogant game, I know. The black waitress who sits on a stool behind a counter and never smiles, talks or makes eye contact, certainly dreams, nice dreams I should think. She only emerges from behind the counter to clear the table when someone departs. She is slow and fatigued in the way she works, as if she cannot really see any point to it. I have tried to thank her but she turns her head away, even though she wasn't looking at me, as if such intercourse were outlawed. There is a German family, a couple with a boy and a girl. They are loud and shout across the room to each other, asking one or the other to bring this or that, the breakfast things laid out on a table in the corner, croissants, bread and coffee. I assume they don't dream, or rather don't remember their dreams, because of course everyone dreams. Even the young English couple must dream. From their accent I assume they're from the North East. He complains all of the time, moaning about what they did the day before, the dreadful food, the boring museums. She reassures him that today will be better. I must have listened to many of their conversations because I know they are here for five days and their ticket includes a full day in Disney Paris, but that isn't until the fourth day. Today his overriding complaint is the hotel. They paid a lot of money and the hotel is dreadful. This morning it was colder than ever and the shower was tepid. I should lean across and agree with them, but immediately become defensive. To my mind, suddenly, the hotel is functional and fine.

The man whom I assume to be the owner sits in a little room adjacent the breakfast room across from the reception and watches television all day. It is loud and intrusive, in the morning a chatty, celebrity news-show. He doesn't talk either, but his expression is more actively uninterested than that of the waitress. Suddenly I like him, and consider him a quirky, interesting character, mildly eccentric and playful. Of course the couple don't know I am English. I hide that as if it needs to be kept secret.

There is also a man on his own. He is well dressed in a suit and tie. He takes his jacket off to eat and rolls up the sleeves of his shirt. I take him to be here on business. He looks as if he is used to travelling, comfortable in his surroundings. When he first appeared at breakfast, which was on my second day, the coffee machine with its confusing little plastic packets and slots presented him with no problem at all. He is fair haired, gentle looking but with strong arms, his forearms when he rolls up his sleeves muscular, with a light golden down of hair. He can't dream, he is too self-assured. Of course the whole thing is preposterous and I am making the most outrageous judgements. All of their dreams may be lofty and noble and only mine in the gutter.

107

I have to get on, put the lives of this grubby little hotel out of my mind and do what I came to do. I sweep all of the crumbs I have made onto a napkin and screw it up. There are no plates with breakfast just napkins. I don't like to leave any mess. I presume it's an English thing, a desire to be unnoticed. I push back my chair, which scrapes along the plastic flooring, and move away. I bump straight into the man who has also stood. He is evidently getting more coffee and thankfully the cup he is holding is empty. "I'm sorry," I say, but then correct myself, saying, "I'm sorry, I mean, pardon, pardonnez moi," my voice flustered, which is concern about the language skill on offer.

He smiles warmly, and quietly says: "Sorry is quite all right, though really not needed."

"Sorry."

He continues to smile and steps towards the coffee machine which is a few feet away from his table. As he inserts his pack of coffee into the slot he turns to me and repeats: "Really not needed." When I reach the door he calls to me and says he hopes I have a good day.

I turn back and say: "I don't suppose I will, but thank you." I immediately feel I have been too disclosing and rush away. I pass the owner in front of his television. He is laughing out loud which is unusual. He turns to me as I pass and is still laughing. I find it unsettling. That must be how paranoia starts, a chance happening: a word, a piece of laughter, a naked figure in a mirror. Reason hangs on a thread.

It is cold outside, snow flurries in the air, flakes singular and discernible. The sky is low and grey, dense with cloud. It could snow heavily, though I think it unlikely. I have reached the conclusion that snow is endangered, an experience that my grandchild might not have. But what would I do if it does snow heavily and I am stranded here? I suppose it wouldn't matter. I am not a real tourist and I have no job I need to return to. I would simply waste money which I don't care about. My mind is torn between a desire for snow, to know that it is still possible, even if only on foreign soil, and the desire to be warm again. I haven't felt so cold for such a long time. Is it really as cold as I think or is it just a state of mind? I look around. Everyone else looks cold. It makes them miserable and insular. This is not a Paris I recall. It is ashen and faded, old and in need of rejuvenation. Perhaps Paris is a state of mind.

It is a short walk to Rue du Faubourg St Honoré and the offices of the British Consul. I have grossly miscalculated and am way before my allotted appointment. I make my way to the Jardin des Tuileries to pass the time. At the gates of the Place de la Concorde are a crowd of women begging. One approaches me with her hands held in supplication, her expression pained, her voice wailing quietly but relentlessly. There is a caravan selling crepes a few feet away. I wonder how they stand this row of misery. Do they just assume it all a sham, a piece of contemporary street theatre? I suppose I do myself, but nevertheless reach into my bag and give more than is sensible – though sensible by what standard, I'm not sure. To my disappointment there is no gratitude, in fact scarcely any acknowledgement. She simply moves on to the next customer, still wailing with grief. I want to say to her that if she is quiet for a moment and listens to the breeze, the snow flecked breeze, she will hear another voice wailing with grief. There are so many layers of reality it is bewildering. Yes my voice is on the breeze, as are the notes of a tune played by piano and violin, like sadness and joy rolled into one, together making something new.

I don't go very far into the Jardin. My business isn't here. Besides it is dreary in this weather, and the damp gravel is marking my shoes, which being delicately woven slippers are entirely unsuitable. I turn back unable to contemplate this place I have only ever known in summer sunlight. I have a very clear memory of sitting here and talking with John, a confessional conversation about my father, an account of a violent man, an account of why London became home. In the summer sunshine he wrapped me up in an enormous hug of new beginnings, confirming me as Louise the artist, the Londoner, freed of a dirty, squalid childhood. This city of holidays and romance haunts me at every corner. Snow and sunshine contend. I am a dancer between the two. I turn and make my way back to the Place de la Concorde. I remember walking here one Sunday morning, the first time we had stayed together in the city, a plush hotel on Boulevard Haussmann, and knowing that everything about life was correct. There was music in my head that morning too, a pop song, scarcely worth remembering now. The same beggar woman accosts me at the gates. I quite angrily tell her that I have already given her a reasonable donation – I call it a donation – but she wails on regardless. I sweep past disgusted by something, something too complex to understand. There were no beggars in my Sunday memory.

At the corner of Rue de Rivoli I bump into the man from breakfast, though not literally this time.

He stops me, laughs and says: "I thought it was a bigger city than this."

"Yes," I say, perturbed by the encounter. I am waiting

to see someone from the Consulate, whilst dreaming of holidays and hidden things, and I find it difficult to find my voice.

"Are you shopping?" he asks. I shake my head. "Heading off to the Louvre?"

"No, no, I'm not."

He smiles and shrugs slightly, questioningly. It is commonplace inquisitiveness, not prying. I shouldn't be so guarded. "I have an appointment, but I'm early. I'm just killing time."

He looks at his watch as if trying to calculate whether he has any time to kill too and then invites me for a drink, tea, coffee, whatever. He says he knows a nice tea-room. For some reason I say I don't know, forcing him to insist. Finally I concede, saying it would be nice. It really would be nice.

He brings me a cup of Earl Grey tea in a glass cup and puts it in front of me. The café is very contemporary with near abstract, but evidently tropical prints, where the serving staff are all young, loud, seemingly happy and incredibly friendly with the customers. There is English music in the background. "I'm sorry," he says, as he takes his seat beside me. "I didn't mean to pry into your business."

"It's really not needed," I say, trying to smile, but knowing that I probably look awkward, at variance to what I'm saying.

He laughs and says: "Good, I like that. You have a good memory."

"It wasn't a lifetime ago."

"Breakfast?"

I smile, more casually than before. He picks up nuance, the fact that there is a dialogue going on with the self as well, a rough, cynical dialogue. "Yes, breakfast. I can remember what was said so long ago."

"And it's not needed to pry or to apologize?"

"Apologize, of course, apologize."

He purses his lips, amused and satisfied. "I'm here on business too."

"I guessed."

"Why, because I'm on my own?"

"Shirt and tie, confidence."

"Confidence?"

"You know, the language, a foreign city. You look at home."

"I get by."

"I say that all of the time. *Je me debrouille*, but I don't get by nearly as well as I did once."

"We're still talking about the language."

"Yes, the language, I mean the language. I don't speak as well as I once did."

"It's just a matter of practice."

"I think there's more to it."

"Like what?"

"It's too personal to say."

"I'm sorry," he says, and holds his hands up in apology, as if he has touched something he really shouldn't have. I must have seen the gesture innumerable times, but never before with such clarity.

"It really is not needed," I say, tired with the joke, but quite taken by his humility.

"No, I think in that instance it perhaps was needed. I probably shouldn't say this but you do seem troubled, troubled by something. You don't have to say anything, you don't even have to nod or shake your head, but if I can help in anyway."

112

"Why?"

"Why?"

"Yes, why should you want to help?"

"Do I need a reason?"

"I think so."

"Well, I'm sorry about that. I don't know, the English abroad, helping each other, which is arbitrary, I admit. I'm here on business but I do have time on my hands, which I also admit. And maybe I wouldn't offer if you weren't so attractive, which I also admit. I also admit to being a fairly decent guy with no reasons in the world."

"I'm sorry, no, I really am."

"I think we have to stop this," he says, smiling, yet at the same time with his eyebrows arched, creating a comically aggrieved gesture.

"Yes, I think you're right."

"So, if I can help, well, just say."

I say that he can't help, in fact that I don't desire any help, but I go on to tell him that my son is dead, died in France in circumstances that haven't been explained and that I have an appointment in the Consulate to discuss it. He listens with patience and sympathy, maybe even something beyond sympathy, which I would call compassion. He says: "I really am terribly sorry, which I know we agreed to stop saying, but I am. I can't imagine what you're going through. If you'd like someone to come with you, not to be involved but just be with, then just say."

"Thank you, that's kind actually, but no. I'll manage, manage quite well, thank you. In fact, I'd better be going." I'm aware that I've only drunk half of my tea, but I have to leave, my emotional walls are beginning to erode and I can't have that, not now, not so close to the appointment.

He stands as I stand. "Good luck," he says. "Look, if

113

you're up to it, let me take you to dinner, tonight. If you want to share what was said then I'll listen, if not we'll just talk."

"I don't know," I respond vaguely.

"I'll knock on your door at seven and if you're ready then we'll do it, and if you're not we won't, without any need for an apology. Don't decide now." I shrug and nod, but say nothing. I make to leave. He calls: "I really do hope it goes well." I nod again, but still say nothing.

Chapter Ten

I am taken into an office by Jason, who doesn't supply any other name and who seems a very junior figure to me. He has a pleasant but bored face, clean and smooth, unmarked by experience. His hair is longer than I would have expected of someone in an official position. In fact, I don't know what his position is and don't think he said. He could be anyone, but he has access to me, to the things that concern me. The office is old, surviving from a former era, with glass fronted bookcases and a large wooden desk. Jason is brisk and buoyant, ushering me to sit whilst he takes his own place. It suggests to me that he doesn't expect this to take long. He gives a cursory look to the file in front of him, spreads his arms wide across the desk and smiles at me genially, as if that is the right thing to do, then asks what he can do for me.

I smile in return, bemused by the question and bemused by him. I am disappointed by the age of Jason and his evident lack of seniority. Of course I am judging him, but already he has betrayed an absence of protocol in dealing with the bereaved. His voice is at a pitch that it would be for any interview, his interest and manner the same. He has no idea about grief. So far he must have been spared; lucky, I suppose.

"My son, my son died in France."

"Some months ago, I believe."

"Yes, some months ago."

"I am sorry for your loss, of course."

"Yes, thank you."

"I don't think I can supply you with any information that you won't already have."

"But I don't have any information," I say without undue emotion. I want to add his name – I don't have any information Jason – but it seems slightly absurd. Strange how absurdity interferes with solemnity.

"Well, let me see."

"He was run over."

"Yes, a road traffic accident."

"Three times."

"Yes, I believe his body was unfortunately not seen in the dark."

"How is that possible?"

He tries not to smile, but doesn't quite succeed. "The dark is the dark Mrs Tennant."

"But how would a driver not be aware of going over a body. I don't believe that is possible."

Jason purses his lips, seemingly concerned on my behalf, clearly working out a line of least resistance. "The police have thoroughly investigated the incident and have no reason to believe anything other than that it was a tragic accident."

"Three times, Jason, he was run over three times, and the police did not conduct a thorough investigation, they said there was nothing to investigate."

"It was a terrible accident."

"You don't believe it, do you? Tell me the truth, Jason."

"I believe there was an accident."

"You think I'm mad."

"A mother."

"You think he was out for kicks."

"I think he was young."

"My son."

"Yes."

"I want to believe something. I want to believe something good."

Jason looks perturbed, out of his depth, but doesn't flounder. He smiles at me. 'I don't know Mrs Tennant, I can only describe to you and explain what official reports say. I wasn't there and you weren't there."

"But you will have formed an opinion of him, a judgement."

"No, I assure you I haven't. Why should I?"

"The report isn't true." He looks at me steadily, deliberately allowing a note of impatience to enter his expression. He shrugs mildly, indicating that I'm straying onto things that are really not his business. It is obvious he is not going to respond. "What about the people he was with? Has anyone spoken to them?"

"I believe he was living with a girl for a while, but there is no way of knowing where she ended up. On the face of it your son had no fixed abode."

"My son is not like that, not how he is being painted."

"I am not responsible for that Mrs Tennant."

"I didn't say you were, I'm just saying that my son wasn't like that."

"Like what, Mrs Tennant?"

I feel cornered, led there by myself. Yes, indeed, not like what? Was he good, was he bad, was he indifferent? And really, should it make any difference to his dying what he was? I am being asked to review my memory, recreate the past and judge something in the present from that review. I am being indulged as a grieving mother, a blind, indiscriminate mother who refuses the truth for

117

the sake of something pedestrian and rubbished anyway. I don't want my child mired. So, if he was good would his death then be palatable? And if being bad reduces the sympathy and dread is it a case of judgement and punishment we are dealing with. It is all hearsay.

I blurt out: "I just don't believe."

"I don't think anyone would expect it of you Mrs Tennant."

"But you didn't know him Jason."

"No Mrs Tennant, obviously not."

"Drugs were his profession not his pastime."

"Mrs Tennant the toxicology report is quite unambiguous. There were quantities of alcohol and drugs in your son's body."

"No Jason, no. You have it all wrong," I say, aware of the rising distress and panic in my voice.

"I'm not saying it Mrs Tennant, I'm just telling you what the toxicology report states to be fact."

"There are no facts, facts can't exist."

Jason closes the file. He obviously feels the subject is closed and there is nothing more to say. He must have judged that we have reached the point where we are now going around in circles, the circle of grief and unreasonable doubts. I can't leave it here, allow him to shuffle me out into anonymity. "Look Jason, his body was run over three times, found on a remote road miles from anywhere. There must be grounds for investigation somewhere in that."

"It is an issue for the French police and they don't feel the case warranted investigation."

"The case?"

"Yes Mrs Tennant, the case."

"My son."

118

He purses his lips and shrugs. He puts both hands, palm down, on the file and says: "I believe you were involved yourself in a road traffic accident."

"That was a long time ago."

"Quite so. I understand that someone died."

"Yes someone died, a child died. I ran into a child who had got off a school-bus and then ran in front of the bus and out into the road."

"Yes, I know."

"How do you know?"

"We have to be thorough Mrs Tennant, that's all."

There is a period of silence. Jason breathes deeply through flared nostrils a number of times and I sit quietly, rebuked, defeated, the wound open, the wound that has never closed, gaping, raw. Eventually I whisper: "I was found to be entirely innocent."

"Oh yes, Mrs Tennant, I know, I wasn't suggesting anything else, not at all. But something like that must be difficult."

"Difficult?"

"To live with."

"Yes something like that is difficult to live with. I don't think a day goes by that I don't think about it, don't think about the things someone can't do but should be able to. Of course that's difficult."

"You were on your way to see your boyfriend I understand."

"I was inexperienced. I had just passed my test."

"Yes, of course, but to overtake a bus. I understand that you have never gone back to live at home."

"London is my home."

"Yes, of course."

"Why have you brought all of this up?"

119

"Have you not thought yourself that someone, some-one like yourself with something like that in the back-ground, might be inclined to read more into something than there really is?"

"No."

"It is possible though."

"No, this is entirely different."

"I am really sorry Mrs Tennant but we are dealing with a tragic accident contributed to by the use of alcohol and drugs."

"There is a piece of music goes over and over in my head, *Spiegel im Spiegel*. I can't get it to stop." He signals vagueness, incomprehension. "It is there for a reason."

For him the interview is over. He tidies his one file, stands and offers me his hand. His hand is surprisingly small and decidedly moist. He says that if he can be of any further help then I shouldn't hesitate to call. I might say that he hasn't been of any help at all but that would be unkind. I am not unkind, just a murderer, a child mur-derer. I suppose I should be grateful he is willing to take my hand, let alone talk to me.

I am shown out by a young woman, charming and exquisite the way they are. In the street it is cold and bright. There is no likelihood of snow now at all.

Chapter Eleven

I had no intention of accepting his invitation to dinner – whoever he is, I don't even have a name – but as the time approaches it seems really quite welcome. I spent the long afternoon wandering through endless streets, stopping at cafés and drinking coffee after coffee, until my nerves were jangling and my body felt as if it were charged with excess electricity. Some streets felt like havens, rows of small, clean shops where people had come out of their flats to buy items for lunch or dinner, streets where people obviously lived.

Of course even the thought of taking pleasure in such quarters was charged with hypocrisy. Jason had underlined something that I have always known – there is no pleasure to be had. Every commonplace is overwritten with the fact that it is a commonplace that someone else can't have, someone else dead at my doing, everything fouled and soiled. With some spirit and pleasure he had put the case for a moral universe. Everything has a cost. And the price I have to pay for doing terrible wrong, evidently, is to be disallowed from asking what has happened to my son. But that doesn't make sense. If Joseph is the price of my wrong doing then the universe must be designed just for me, but that is nonsense. The universe is equal, each of its parts equal. Joseph, or for that matter John, are not part of my balance-sheet. But then I am culpable.

So it went, on and on.

Eventually I came back to the hotel. The owner said something to me that I failed to grasp but I laughed, laughed as if I'd really got the joke. He could have been delivering bad news, but I didn't think so. Back in my room I did nothing, went from bed to window, switched on the television and turned it off. There is a brown stain on the carpet beneath the radiator. The radiator obviously leaks. The room smells constantly damp. In summer with the windows open, the air dry and hot, the noise of the street filling the room, it would be an entirely different place. I would read my world differently. I am trapped in dampness and cold and inertia and guilt.

I never was guilty. Witnesses said how the boy ran across the front of the bus without looking, right into the path of the oncoming vehicle. Louise Shore who was driving the vehicle, her father's who scarcely drove it himself, was not at fault. Except Louise Shore, coming to the end of her A levels, an artist who hung around with boys in bands, in pubs where bands played, headstrong and truculent, was not only inexperienced but impatient. She gave no thought to anyone bursting across the road in front of the bus, which she should have done, because that's what happened. She knows how much she wanted to get to her guitarist in the band boyfriend whose parents were out. She knows the feisty, painted up, angry teenager that was driving. She knows it forever. She knows the scream of brakes, the crunching thud of collision, the unimaginable damage. She knows that you cannot run over a body and not know that you have done it. She refuses to accept that the guilty are debarred the rights of the moral universe. Louise Tennant knows she was

122

steered away but doesn't know why. She is floundering in the dark but will keep on.

At precisely seven o'clock he knocks on the door, a confident but not insistent knock. When I open the door he smiles casually, warmly, putting neither too much nor too little into it. He raises his hands in an easy questioning manner. I am dressed for the occasion but decline. He steps closer. He half-whispers: "I said I wouldn't insist, but seeing you now I think I really want to. It won't do any harm and we will be company for each other. Of course, if you'd rather stay in your sumptuous room, then by all means pass up a perfectly innocent dinner arrangement." He smiles again and looks frankly boyish.

"I don't know your name," I say.

He shrugs and says: "You can call me Bill." Does that mean it isn't his name, but an alias brought out for tonight's dinner? Why should he need an alias if everything is so innocent? Besides why does he assume that the issue is innocence whereas, in fact, the issue is guilt? He goes on: "I'm sure there are all sorts of things you don't know, and lots of things you wouldn't be bothered to know, but over dinner you could just ask."

"Yes, I suppose so. Yes, you may be right."

"I don't know your name, but I don't insist on it."

"My name? My name is Louise, Louise Tennant. I put a lot of store by names."

"Why? A name is just a name." I shake my head, but don't want to get into it, wrangling about such personal material. He continues, his voice still tending towards a whisper: "Are you persuaded, Louise?" I must look mystified because he smiles and adds: "Dinner. Shall we dine together?"

"Oh yes, why not."

"Do you have somewhere in mind or would you like me to choose?" I shake my head. I am playing the traditional role. I will be led. Tonight that is what I want. "Vegetarian?" he asks, presumably checking whether I am or not, not whether that is what I would choose. I smile and shake my head. "I thought you might be."

"Why?"

"Being an artist, I suppose. Oh, I don't know."

"I never said I was an artist. How do you know I am an artist?"

"I don't," he says and smiles. "I meant artistic. You strike me as artistic."

"A type, you mean."

"We are all types."

"I thought we were all individuals."

"Types of."

The idea makes me laugh. In the invention of Louise Tennant, the escapee, guilty of several crimes, only one major, I overlooked the likelihood of vegetarianism. My diet is cosmopolitan– though largely cheese and wine of late – but not absolutely moral. I am red in tooth and claw. He looks pleased with my laughter without looking pleased with himself. I warm to that. "I would like traditional French cuisine."

"Of course."

We walk to the restaurant which is not very far away. I'm sure he knew all along where he intended to go. It is modern, the frontage different to the rest of the street, glass and brass, the inside uncluttered and clean. John and I tend towards the old, drawn by turn-of-the-twentieth century style and architecture; a time of possibility, John always says. I think in terms of art and agree. We so naturally agree, bringing together two strands of the same confirmation. Looking back I feel that we even divide the language between us and I am now missing his half of it. With John it would all make sense.

I tell Bill what I want and let him order. He speaks extremely well. I compliment him on it, but below the surface I'm rather piqued that he does. He is a business man and it is the business men who speak well these days. There is something obviously snobbish about my irritation. He is incredibly comfortable in himself. When the wine comes he asks me to taste it which surprises me. I feel I am being teased. Does he assume I don't recognize and relish quality, the artist only aspiring to excess? In fact I recognize it, relish it and would drink it to excess. Tonight, though, I will be careful. I tell the waiter it is very good, articulating my words with ease, determined not to be outdone. Of course it is a particularly simple phrase. Le vin, c'est tres bon, merci.

He holds up his glass says cheers and then asks: "How did you get on today?"

"Today," I respond evasively, without knowing why, "today I wasted my time. I wandered around for much of the day and overdosed on coffee."

"I meant with your appointment, but if you'd rather not talk about it, that's fine. Tell me something about the sights of Paris."

"I'm sorry."

He smiles: "It's really not needed, and I promise that's the last time I'll say that tonight, the last time I'll say it ever."

I smile in return. There is something so self-effacing about him, despite his obvious comfort. I suppose he isn't showing off, play-acting the alias Bill, but being whoever he is. He's right about the phrases we are building up between us, they should be dispensed with, they are too personal. John and I have so many phrases that bond us, lock us together in the same intimate history, lines picked up from other people and made into our jokes. The primary school teacher who said of Joseph and his friend when they had written on the toilet wall, *You don't know what they're thinking*, which we seized on voraciously, they becoming the whole strange, cluttered world. I loved it when John winked, one time he was putting Joseph's sheets in the washer, and said: *You don't know what they're leaking*. And now I don't think John knows what I'm thinking, the raw, anticipatory love I still grudge him with. What wouldn't I give to have John opposite me now? But, of course, we wouldn't be in this restaurant at all. Bill is a much bigger man than John, though without the veneer of protection. He might be able to fight for a woman in time honoured style, but I doubt whether he would know how to protect one. I say over in my head for my own pleasure: You don't know what they're thinking. I smile appreciatively for myself. Bill accepts it as his without question.

"So, tell me," he says, "what would you recommend I do not miss in the cultural life of Paris."

I shrug. "I don't know what your likes and dislikes are."

"I could make a fool of myself now, but will just say I know what I like when I see it."

"I intend to see the Picasso Museum and the Centre Georges Pompidou."

"I confess I have never been."

"You should, maybe you will see something you like very much."

126

He smiles sceptically, yet confidentially: "Yes, I might, you never know. If you don't mind maybe we could go together." I don't instantly respond but look at him, wondering about the invitation, the expression with which he asked it. He is a perplexing combination of confidence and doubt. "Sorry, I didn't mean to impose myself on you. You obviously like to do these things alone."

"No I don't," I say plainly. "I do them alone. Of course it would be very pleasant to go together, but do you not have business to see to?"

"I am in Paris," he responds with a mild flourish, "I deserve at least one day's grace. But be warned, I know absolutely nothing about art in any of its forms."

"Is that true?"

"Yes it's true."

"You're probably wrong. You must have been touched by song and dance, everyone is."

"Oh yes," he responds with mild, comic determination, "I've been a hit on the dance floor, master of jazz fusion and soul."

I smile, and again look at him, wondering about the clearly self-mocking expression, the ever so slightly hopeless undertone. I eat some of my starter, which has been sitting untouched for a while. The taste is exquisite, crab with apricot mayonnaise served with julienne vegetables and flowers drizzled with truffle oil. I can't remember the last time I ate such food. I drink more wine and rediscover the relationship of wine and food. I can't deny the pleasure I feel. I eat some more and then put down my knife and fork and say: "I wasn't being evasive earlier. Today was a waste of time. I learnt nothing new."

"Did you expect to?"

"I don't know."

"What exactly was said?"

I eat a bit more. He waits, opting not to apologize for his question, true to his word. I swallow and drink another mouthful of wine. He refills my glass, his own scarcely touched. "I presume they think me a grief stricken, crazy mother, when in fact I am a grief stricken, crazy mother."

"My turn. Is that true?"

"Grief stricken, yes, crazy, probably."

"Why crazy?"

"Because a tune keeps going round and round in my head, *Spiegel im Spiegel*."

"Mirror in mirror."

"Yes."

"A real tune, you mean?"

"Oh yes, a real tune, a real, very beautiful tune, but somehow it's telling me that something is not quite right, something is altogether wrong. Is that crazy?"

"Yes, I would have thought so, but it doesn't mean it's wrong."

"No, maybe not. I was fobbed off, but why?"

"Are you sure?"

"No, of course not. The young man might have been doing his best to humour an insane, wounded mother. I don't know."

"So what now?"

"I don't know. I've got a number, a girl. I should have rung her by now but I keep putting things off. The person who gave me the number was nervous. I keep coming across people who are nervous. I sometimes think I'm making them up, not them as such, but how they are, because it doesn't make sense. It must be the way I'm looking at them."

"Just a number, not a name."

I look at him again without responding. He is comfortable with that now. We have progressed from having any need to apologize. It suggests that big steps have been taken. Strangers apologize, intimates rarely do. I speak very slowly, as if meditating on it, which I'm not. "Yes, just a number, no name. Someone gave me a number and said it was the number of a friend of Joseph's."

"Someone handed it to you, you mean."

"No, no, it was a message on the phone, left for me, but no name."

I smile, wondering why I am lying so much. I don't trust myself, don't trust my motives or my behaviour. Am I dramatizing everything, enlisting him, because the truth is maybe as they said? I certainly have no intention of telling him that my son was under the influence of drugs and alcohol.

As if he has read my mind he says: "I know it's none of my business, and tell me that's the case if you want, but you haven't said how your son died, just that the circumstance were unusual."

I let his words percolate through me for a while, taking the opportunity to drink some more. He is very patient and doesn't force any response from me. At the same time his inquiry hangs there demanding an answer. He makes it so it can't be ignored. I'm struggling to find the right words to convey what is strange without it reflecting badly on Joseph. The strangeness is Joseph. He left his wife and child, his occupation which he loved, and his body contained drugs and alcohol. He was run over, three times, in the dark. And that is the only strangeness I am left with. He was run over three times in the dark, and no one is comfortable talking about it. And I was given a

129

name and a number. Who on earth would be comfortable talking about the death of a child with the grief ravaged mother? "He was run over in a village, miles from Paris, miles from where he was living, run over three times, and I know it sounds crazy but there is something not right about it."

"Look, if you want any help, I don't know what, talking to the girl, I don't know, anything, just say?"

"Did I say it was a girl?"

He smiles warmly, sympathetically, amused: "Yes, you did."

"I suppose I must have."

"Louise, I don't know what has happened, and you tell me just whatever you want, but trust me, really."

"Nothing's happened to me, it's just that things don't make sense. Sorry, maybe I should go."

"No," he says without aggression, but decisively, "you'll eat your dinner."

I acquiesce with a brief nod, gratefully I think. I sit back, determined to speak no more about Joseph. I have no right to burden Bill with it. I look around the restaurant, its tables lit discreetly in silver dulled light. No one is sitting in silence. Of course the French are great talkers, presumably happy with cold food, which they consume slowly in the very brief pauses between speaking. I imagine what it would be like now at this precise moment if someone walked in with a machine-gun and started shooting indiscriminately. There would be mayhem and pandemonium, and then the stillness of corpses. In my narrative the gunman then shoots himself, for convenience sake I suppose. There would be so many endings, but also so many beginnings. Why was the English woman, a married woman, mother of a dead child dining with

130

a man who went by the alias of Bill? Why was anyone with anyone? And of course we would be missing from all future presence. The same woman would be doomed forever never to unearth the mystery of her dead child. Bill's real name would probably be discovered, but his undemonstrative confidence would be missing from the world.

Every commonplace is marred by the fact that someone can't experience it. It isn't the first time I've had such a thought, it is in fact quite commonplace for me. The first time was whilst watching Joseph on stage with a tea-towel on his head in a nativity play in the part, naturally, of Joseph. It was a wonderful performance, six year olds performing as if they were in a Japanese Noh play, big expressions, moments in time, brief staggered lines. I thought of the smiling faces in Nazi news-reel, thought of the way such innocence is up for grabs, and felt so fortunate. And then I thought, what if someone strolled in and blew it all away. The image is devastating, the smiling child, and then the silence of corpses. My whole being crumbles at the thought. I hear the scream of brakes, the noise of collision, the silence of corpses. There is no escape, no redemption.

Bill breaks into my reverie: "Your fish is going cold."

"Oh yes, of course, but I think the French like food cold."

He shrugs and smiles, really having no opinion on the subject.

"You've been quiet for a while," he says halfway through the main course – cutlets of sea bass and salmon served with two separate sauces and a mould of rice and a mould of pureed green vegetables – "is everything all right?"

"Of course, it couldn't be nicer."

"Not just the fish."

I look at him again, unsure how to answer, probably unsure of the question. Yes, I am all right, though my imagination engages with the highly destructive. "Women," I say, "you don't know what they're thinking." I immediately balk at what I've said. It smacks of disloyalty. I want to retract, but existence isn't like that. The deed cannot be undone, and damage is so easily effected. I hope he makes nothing of it, but that is a vain hope.

He laughs out loud and says: "When you don't they get annoyed and when you do they go crazy."

I smile, pleased that he overdid it, cancelling out what I'd said. "Everything is nice, thank you," I say.

"You didn't say whether you wanted me to help with anything, talking to the girl for instance."

"Maybe, I don't know that I will."

"Of course, do whatever feels right, and only you can know what that is."

I give a circumspect nod but say nothing. The wine bottle is empty, I'm pretty sure that I drank most of it. As I'm working it out the waiter replaces it with another. I didn't see it being ordered. Of course I've drunk too much to know how to stop. What am I in danger of being, maudlin or fun?

Without fully realizing it I begin to cry. Suddenly I am aware of the restaurant again. Bill is smiling, calmly, looking at me, unperturbed. "I'm sorry," I say, hazarding the catch-phrase that has become ours.

"I think it's been an emotional day for you. You're taking on too much alone."

I can't answer. I want to go. Suddenly I feel

desperately tired and I want to sleep. I make to move. Bill stays me for a moment, telling me he'll pay first and then we'll go. I fish around in my bag insisting that I pay half. He won't hear of it, adding that it won't be put down to expenses either, he wouldn't want to sully the evening in any way. I don't really know what he's saying.

He has his arm around me and supports me all the way back to the hotel. I am aware of everything, but it all has that wonderful speed and imprecision of intoxication. I know what is happening but can't control events. All I can do is look. He collects both of our keys and guides me to the lift. He leads me to my door and puts the key in the lock for me. I suppose this is the moment. I don't know what will happen, or what I want to happen. I have no volition. If he comes into the room with me I don't know how I will respond. In truth I ache for him to come into the room with me and equally I can't bear for it to happen.

"Goodnight, Louise," he says, and he lifts his hand and trails his fingers down my cheek, his touch as delicate as feathers. "I don't know what you're going through, but I can see that it's hell. I'm a widower so maybe I know a bit of it, but I wouldn't claim more. Try to sleep, tomorrow you have to teach me all there is to know about Art." He pushes open my door and ushers me through. He takes out the key and puts it into my hand, wrapping my fingers around it, whilst telling me to keep it safe. The door closes behind me and I'm standing in the cold and dank room. I begin to cry, noiselessly but painfully. It is too cold to undress. I wrap a gown tightly around me and crawl beneath the covers. I expect to fall straight to sleep but instead lie there listening to the sounds of the street, disconnected, remote sounds, forming shapes and then collapsing. It seems to go on all of the night, but I assume some of it is dreaming.

Chapter Twelve

The sounds of the hotel wake me, water rushing through pipes, cisterns flushed, the watery start to the day. The room is as cold as ever. There are televisions playing, loud enough to be audible, but not loud enough to be understood. I am sick of having to work so hard just to understand, worn-out by it. Today I am to be escorted, so I will be able to share the burden. The thought is pleasing, soothing even. I wish I had slept better. I want to be good company, attractive, not washed out with dark, sunken eyes. My vanity shocks me. I am so wrapped up I feel as if I am in a strait-jacket, but moving is uncomfortable, cold and damp. I am still dreaming, my mind in so many places at once, in the street, in the room, in unknown regions. My mind is in my body, my body is in the world, the world is in a hall of mirrors, I am inside a hall of mirrors, the tune signals my confusion. I need to get on, ground myself. I have a date. The thought flatters and frightens me. The televisions crackle in the air, impossible to locate.

He knocks at eight fifteen precisely. I call out telling him to wait just a moment. I don't know why because all I do is sit on the side of the bed. I am flustered, marginally breathless. It crosses my mind that I wish I had a drink. The thought lifts me out of my stupor. I am not so far gone – I am a grieving mother, not a dipsomaniac. I open the door wide, already smiling, signalling welcome and anticipation. It is the first time I have seen him not wearing a suit and tie. Casually dressed he looks well: grey polo-shirt, loosely tied scarf, black jeans and boots. Boots! – I must have looked him up and down, head to toe. I ask him to step inside a moment. He crosses the threshold and stands in exactly the same pose as he had outside the door, loose, relaxed, his jacket draped over his arm. I collect a few things and put them in my bag. He comments on the fact that the room is freezing. I say that I assumed all the rooms were cold. His room is perfectly warm and recommends that I report it; my radiator is obviously not working properly. His advice is so obvious I wonder why I never thought of it. It is evident that I need advice; I'm not seeing things clearly.

When we go down to breakfast he mentions it on my behalf. The owner stands up and deserts his television for a moment and genuinely apologizes. I find his attention uncomfortable. He will be jumping to conclusions. I don't know why I am so uncomfortable with that but I am. I wave away his need to apologize. I think I object to the fact that I seem more real in his eyes with a man than I did without. Is that just impertinence or something more fundamental? He and Bill talk some more after I have gone ahead into the breakfast room.

Bill wants tea and presumes I do, Earl Grey the same as yesterday. There is something mildly absurd about it as if he's showing me how comfortable he is taking charge, demanding something not obviously on offer, coffee the norm. However, I agree and say that tea would be lovely. He calls over the woman who clears the tables and asks for tea, Earl Grey. She makes no comment but goes off and returns with two cups of boiling water with a tea bag each on a saucer. He watches me as I eat and drink, his lips parting and coming together, his eyes fixed on me. I can't guess what he's thinking. He certainly isn't uncomfortable, doesn't find any need to talk, to entertain me. I find it all unnerving, the scrutiny, the apparent patience, the ease. I am not used to a man like this. My trust in men is built around John, his gentle care: except he's in America and I'm here. I know I have croissant all over my lips. It seems that at our most vulnerable we let ourselves down. I certainly feel that I am letting myself down. For a moment, catching the unguarded intensity of his interest, I feel stripped of dignity. The moment hurts and matters. I feel a welling of tears. I am being unfaithful, unjust to my husband and I really don't know why. I tell myself that this is about me, not him, but, of course, that is a lie. I stop eating and carefully wipe my mouth intending to tell Bill that the museum trip is off.

He must sense that something is coming and anticipates me: "How did you sleep?" he asks.

I consider whether my response should be honest or small-talk and opt for the former. "I slept like a mummy, wrapped up in layers, cold and dazed."

"A mummy?" he questions, and cocks his head in a pleasant half-smile. He is wise enough to pick up such a simple pun. Yes, a mummy, bandaged but not healing, bandaged but dead to the core. I have no answer to give, other than to return the half-smile. "So have you thought anymore about what you'll do next?" I shake my head. "The offer is always there, any help I can give, really."

"I know. It's kind. I'm struggling to work it out."

"All right."

He finally looks away, the lines of his face instantly relaxing as if his thought patterns have altered. I never have to wonder what John is thinking, which doesn't

137

remove mystery from him simply makes everything easeful. I am not competent enough for this encounter. I would escape if I could, but already it's too late for that.

Outside it's as cold as ever, though still it doesn't actually snow, just flakes and flurries. Bill takes my arm and laces it through his, taking charge of me. The gesture is warming, satisfying yet uncomfortable.

Bill looks amused in the Centre George Pompidou. On the ground floor there is a temporary exhibition called Reflections. The work is varied: shrunken heads, blurred images, video clips (one of someone shivering continuously), anatomical shapes, a sequence of hats, face painting for children, distorted mirrors. Art would naturally imitate and mock life. I put my head inside a box and can see all sides of me, profile and back, images public yet personally unknown. I look older than I think, my face patterned with fine lines: lack of sleep, alcohol, nightmares. I remove my head grieving for what the box has so casually removed. Bill chooses this inauspicious moment to demand an explanation, his art lesson.

I shrug and smile, the question he poses is so comical and slightly petulant. "It is about looking, about alteration, not necessarily self-expression. It is about shifting boundaries so that reality is recast. It affects the mind not the eye, abstract rather than narrative ideas. Pure idea, I suppose." I smile, embarrassed by the gravity in my voice. "It's fun as well, reshaping our perceptions, the way we see human form, the motives for dressing the human body in the ways we do. It's about ways of seeing." He smiles and nods, then throws up his hands in mock surrender.

"And does it matter if it exists?" he asks.

"What do you mean?"

"Does it really contribute anything to human knowledge? Does it improve the world, or lessen it, or do anything to it?"

"This or any art?"

"I suppose I just wonder what knowledge actually is. What is it we want kids to grow up knowing? This is aimed at kids isn't it?" I shrug. It's for anyone. He goes on. "I just wonder what message this would give to any kid."

"To think and feel."

"But that's not knowledge, not knowing. So what should we insist is the minimum of knowing? What could we extract from the sum of human knowing without catastrophe? Would a world without Plato, Maimonides, Descartres, Spinoza, Bach, Beethoven, the Bible and Talmud, the prophets, the Messianic idea, stuffed heads, shrunken heads, tiny heads, bullet heads, be any the worse off?"

"It would be impoverished."

"Would it? Is this helping to feed the world, solve the problem of Palestine old and new, find a cure for disease, solve the problem of the environment? It smacks to me of laughing at people."

His final words are not playful anymore but angry. There is something destructive in his way of seeing. What he doesn't trust he wants to wipe away.

"Art teaches about the need for freedom and the consciousness of freedom. It is spiritual resistance."

He smiles broadly, and breaks away. He takes a few steps, angry steps to my mind, and then stops. He turns back, points at the hats and says: "I like them, I like the hats."

"Yes," I reply, "I like the hats too."

139

"Does it mean anything?"

"If you want it to."

He smiles triumphantly. "Take away the paraphernalia, the treatise, the supportive documents, the protestors, the champions, and there's not much left, is there?"

"I don't know what you mean."

"I mean it makes a virtue out of obscurity, relies on obscurity. It's a con, it really is. I think people deserve something better. This is fad and fashion, not art."

I should be outraged and I am, but I don't want to fight. He is passionate in his rejection, his scepticism. I have to respect that, whilst disliking it. I am used to enthusiasm and complicity. This man is a challenge. His composure has been ruffled. His composure has fallen foul of distrust. It is comical. We have only started. We have the collection of modern art to see. I am outraged and amused. I take him by the hand. I am going to be brave. This is my world. I smile and say: "I think I could put up a good case for macramé, weaving, silk-screen, gouache."

"Of course, but they are skills."

"I'm teasing."

"I know you are. I like it."

I am pretty sure he doesn't like it, but we have found a common ground, debate and discord.

I lead him to the upper floors where I assume we'll carry on in much the same vein. He stops at the top of the escalator and gazes at the skyline of Paris. He asks me if I find it beautiful or not. I think I probably do. He seems satisfied. He says that the one thing the French really know how to do well is to be French. I don't understand, but I'm pretty sure I'll find it offensive so don't ask him to explain.

140

He is rather more subdued and reflective viewing the permanent collection. He asks me questions of meaning and interpretation. He stops in front of the figure of a small squat statue that periodically strikes a gong. The thing amuses him, maybe even fascinates him. He says: "Do you know what makes this art?" What could I say, the inventiveness, the insistence on making someone re-examine space, line and sound making a totality, the play on looking, correspondences and context.

"Because someone bought it, someone was willing to pay the asking price. As soon as it has a cost people think it matters. I actually like the little fellow."

"In many ways you speak like my husband, but different, more cynical I suppose, more pessimistic. Oh I don't know. The same but different."

"Don't get me wrong, I love mankind, it's just that I rather wish I liked it as well." He smiles broadly, so that I don't know whether he's serious or not. His sense of fun is peculiar, I think, personal and peculiar. Even if he isn't serious I think he means something. Maybe that's what it is about him. He loves himself but wishes he liked himself. There is a wound of some kind. Of course there is a wound. He told me he was a widower. I haven't asked. That is remiss of me.

"Tell me about your wife."

"My wife?"

"Yes."

"Why?"

"Because she was married to you. You chose to be married. I don't know. I'm naturally curious."

"There's nothing to say."

"I'm sorry, I didn't mean to pry."

"I don't believe you are, I just have nothing to say or

141

explain. I don't know which bits matter. We were happy, very happy. I know that."

"I'm sorry."

"Yes, I'm sorry too. But at least I know we were happy. But apparently I talk like your husband."

"No nothing like him."

"I stand corrected and don't mind at all. Why isn't he with you?"

What do I say – because my husband has run away, immersed himself in work like the textbook says, leaving me to fend with the strangeness, the intolerable mirrors that reflect nothing but more damned mirrors? But then John knows nothing of this, the terrible stories of his son, the son he believed intolerant, a judgement he can't forgive himself for making. John just isn't here.

"My husband is dead," I say, my voice hushed, devoid of strength.

He gives a barely discernible nod. To my horror I am sure a brief smile passes his lips. He suppresses it, ruthless with himself I feel. He steps up to me and embraces me, loosely, as friends might. He says: "I suppose we were bound to discover each other."

"Like you, I have nothing to say."

"Naturally, I understand that."

He throws up his hands, smiles expansively and says: "Come on, I've had enough of this, let's go and eat."

Over lunch, croque-monsieur in a nearby brasserie, I tell him that I intend to go to the village, see where the crime took place. He picks me up on the word crime but I stand by it. What else if not a crime? Is that not what the music is indicating, the certainty of falsehood, duplicitous acts, criminality.

"Are you sure you should go?" he asks.

142

"Of course, very sure."

"But what good will it do?"

"To see. Seeing might reveal something."

"I think you should think carefully."

"There isn't anything to think about. I'm here. It's something I have to do."

"And if you get hurt?"

"How do you mean, hurt? Who is there to hurt me?"

"Joseph, seeing where the accident happened, putting yourself through that. I think Joseph can hurt you."

"I told you his name was Joseph?"

"Of course."

"It is very sweet the way you care, but you would do the same, I know you would."

"All right, but I'm coming with you."

"No. No, thank you. I want to go alone."

We say no more. Our conversation suggests parting and I don't think we've worked out the nature of that yet. Once again I am entering something as if it were already a memory, over before I know what has begun. But is it a good, bad or indifferent memory? At least there is still that to learn.

Perhaps because I am so entranced, he doesn't object or complain about anything in the Pablo Picasso museum. Maybe it is just the fact that he is in the presence of truly astronomically priced works of art. As an economic proposition it makes sense to him. Over lunch he insisted on wine. Wine at lunch time leaves me floating and remote. I wish I had refused. I want to feel and be concrete, my eye and mind unsullied in the presence of these works. I am immersed in line, colour and texture. They are like so many utterances coming together to form a whole. The work of a single artist brought together is so much more correct than single paintings displayed without context and connection. My looking draws patterns into being, possibilities. I don't want to explain any of this to Bill, don't want to admit to enthusiasm.

I walk around quiet and subdued. I want nothing laid bare. The trouble is grief enters every level of being, prising things apart, exposing the soft underbelly that one tries to conceal. The fantastic visions of Picasso's mind are intruded on with grief and found to be familiar. Every act of creation contains its negation. Creation is fragile. I love it for its fragility: I hate it for the same. Bill looks at my looking, conjuring something. It is inescapable. He smiles, pleased with my pleasure. It is a long time since I saw such an understanding.

I move away, having acknowledged that smile, move away with a growing sense of self-satisfaction. This is art as revolution. And then just as quickly I am emptied out. I stand forlorn. With just a word Bill could snatch away my pleasure and label it sham. I am grateful that he chooses not to, grateful whereas once I would have stood my ground, but the ground is constantly being pulled away from me. Solid earth is a myth. I must have given up my own struggles. It's ironic that Joseph should bring me to this. I always thought it funny how children abandon your struggles. You bring them up without God, but they are not anti-God. You bring them up to respect minority opinion, but they don't campaign. We make something and lose something. I refuse to acknowledge that that is reasonable.

John was always more optimistic. He said every generation eventually found its voice. It was arrived at through crisis and emergency. He refuted any suggestion that Joseph's generation was any more materialistic or trivial than any other. They just have more he said, they don't necessarily want more. I need his wisdom, his belief, his hope. Bill touches my shoulder. I shiver all over, the feeling is one of pleasure and pain. I turn and tell him I've had enough, enough of it all, art and artists.

He suggests tea and a cake. It seems a wonderful idea. He knows a very nice tea-room in the Place Igor Stravinsky. From the tea-room we can see the brightly painted figures around the fountain. In Paris there is no escaping art. The fountain is one fabulous carnival. The tea-room is very English, cosy and quaint. The French are much more sophisticated with tea than the English. I point this out to Bill. He treats me to a speech about the quality of the French. I knew it had to come at some point. He admires the French ability to preserve a concept of being French, unlike the English who are so polite that they give up their identity without a struggle. He insists it is not a matter of race. Anyone can be French, if they are willing to be French.

I don't agree with a single word of this. I would snap all of the bonds and barriers that break us up into individuals and nations. But I say nothing. I have no spirit these days. I am an artist in recollection. I struggle to think what Bill finds of interest in me. I concede and give in so easily. There is no fight in me at all. A mummy through and through.

In the evening we eat in Chartier, a restaurant on the Rue du Faubourg Monmartre. It is my choice. It has been there since 1896. It is a vast old-fashioned hall of a place, where the waiters wear aprons and write your order on the paper table coverings. It is a place of noise and excitement. Whenever I am here with John we always eat in Chartier. I know it is a risk to be here, there is so much invested in it, but I had to come. As soon as I walk in I am flooded and burdened with memory. I can see John. He is in every nuance, his pleasure large and encompassing. It is an error to be here. I am tempted to run, but I don't have the legs for it. I am weak and dilute.

Bill orders as he did the night before. He is making this place his. It doesn't conform to his standard – the food is basic and traditional, though high quality – but it is French. It conforms to his understanding of French identity, so he will accept it on those terms. He smiles a great deal as if there is something celebratory about our being here, celebratory because it is my choice. I am sure he thinks I am drinking in that spirit, whereas I am drinking in pain. When the first bottle is empty – of which I've drunk the greater part – he takes out his mobile phone and suggests we ring the girl. He pronounces the intention as if it is part of the celebratory feel, something reckless and spontaneous. I drop my head. I will not have my tragedy misconstrued, made into a party game. He sees my disgust, if not my distress, and apologizes. We have never really broken the habit of apologizing. We eat in relative quiet, surrounded by eternal noise.

Later, after more wine – I don't know how many cafés – we hesitate outside my room. We have spoken little all evening. I feel adrift. I can't imagine the picture I project. I am a spectre. I am betraying John. I have time on my hands. I am bereaved. Who am I kidding? I want to be fucked. I invite him in. He asks me if I'm sure. I hate him for that. He is making me the main actor. I have to tell him that I'm sure. I unlock the door and lead the way. Much to my surprise the room is warm. It won't be difficult being naked. I take his touch with gratitude and longing. The sex is a struggle, a fight and a victory.

146

Chapter Thirteen

The first thing he says in the morning is that he wants to help me. I find it offensive. It smacks of male arrogance. He evidently fancies himself the saviour and hero of the story: having bedded the widow he'll now sort out the tedious drama of the mother's grief. Well that is not his role. He and I are using each other. He doesn't have a singular desire for Louise Tennant. His desire is habitual. He is an athlete. For him performance is everything. And he's good. I can't complain. He could never comprehend that at times John and I have simply touched, fearlessly wanting to give pleasure, not knowing where body and mind ended. Bill rears up on his arms like a flesh eater. I feel great force, power, but no wonder, no surprise. But John has equipped me for this encounter, taught me trust, this compromise. We do it again, proving it was no fluke, not just the wine. He groans loudly and I wonder why, wonder who it is he wants to overhear. I'm sure for him it is another demonstration of his help. If my counsellor were here, an invited guest sitting at the foot of the bed, he would applaud and say there is strong evidence that I am moving on.

Over breakfast he asks what I want to do today. For a while I don't answer. My mind rests on so many things at once. Breakfast, the act of eating, takes me to John. He is so fastidious. If he were here he would eat so carefully, letting his crumbs land on the napkin, leaving nothing for the woman to collect. Having so little interest in the hotel guests she wouldn't even know he had been here. Bill on the other hand is messy, entirely indifferent to the flaking croissant. It is someone else's concern. If I asked him why he is so lax he would tell me that he isn't the cleaner. He will believe in a definite division of labour based on income not opportunity. Bill navigates the world he sees; John lays bare its construction. I am used to deconstruction. Except, when it is down to me I prove cowardly. I should have rung the number I was given on day one. I have waited. I have been a tourist. I have found myself in a holiday romance, moving on before the story was ready for it. I have failed my duty.

In truth, I have considered the call many times, rehearsed it in my head, planned the first sentence, an efficient French allo followed by the bold statement that I am ringing about Joseph Tennant. But from that moment I will have no further control. No amount of rehearsal can see me beyond that basic beginning. What if I am met by complete incomprehension? Would that mean that my trip is over, everything done, the mystery to remain just that? Or what if she is to tell me more damning facts about my dead boy? Can I take more revelations about him? Of course that is why I haven't yet rung. I can't face the consequences. I don't want the story to finish here, but I don't want to hear any more bad things, and I'm not ready to go home. The latter thought is a terrible admission.

Is it possible that I have never known my own son? I have always seen him with my features, my blood, my thought, but there is so much more in the mix, so many noughts and crosses, things ingested, contaminants, flavour enhancers, insecticides, pesticides, altered DNA, my falsely fuelled boy. For all those years of mother and son was he humouring me, treating me as just another person to dupe, a part of the problem and not the solution. Growing up, of course we never think our parents understand us, neither us nor the world we have no choice but to occupy. We always assume it a more complex, difficult world than theirs. And yet we think we have the right to understand them. My father, the flawed pitiful bully, my mother, the self-effacing victim. In the latter years of her dreadful, doomed marriage she discovered reading, at first romances but then nineteenth century classics. As she read she removed herself, immersed in nineteenth century concerns of legitimacy, inheritance, poverty and wealth. In a solitary, lonely world of her own she discovered so many things, but the more she discovered the more she discovered she didn't have. Any possible joy she felt in her reading was cancelled by joy's absence. Maybe she entered marriage with a younger man playing the role of romantic heroine, one that she had dreamed of for years but never thought could exist and when she miraculously had it probably regretted that it had come so late.

Of course all this is speculation. We never confided like that, never had the shared vocabulary to do it. It was all going to be so different with my children – which for reasons unknown turned out to be only one. We were to be friends and trust in each other. As a parent I was always self-conscious of my own thinking. When I worried I had to be worried for him, not me; when I was disappointed I had to be disappointed for him, not me. He only ever had to be happy. That was the mantra. If he had turned round and said that school was not for him would I have condoned his decision knowing that his options would be reduced? And would it have been right at all? Maybe

149

they have the right to be unhappy as well. Besides, who wants to be a friend of their parents? I was his mother. It is a job. A job I still have to do.

I tell Bill that I don't want to do anything today. I have something I need to do alone. He asks me if I can share this task with him. I tell him he knows fine well how I feel about it. He injects a note of passion into his voice and tells me he wants to help. I shake my head. This is for me to do. He looks furious and remonstrates with me. Surely I owe it to him to let him help. I find his choice of words preposterous. I tell him that I don't owe him anything. He looks crushed, suddenly like an overgrown boy, awkward and uncertain. I should explain that I have to do this alone. I am the mother, a woman, strong in purpose and character. I have grown up believing in women. My destiny lies in this. The music is mine. I make connections. It's what I do.

I say nothing of the sort and instead change the subject and ask him how it is he can afford so much time from work. He shrugs and says it's just the nature of the job. I ask him what it is he does. He shrugs again and says it's just something in import and export. I smile and say he makes it sound mildly criminal. I have succeeded in making him smile. When we part he asks me to keep him informed. He says he cares, wants to help, wants the opportunity. I smile but say nothing except that I'll see him later. He says I will, emphasising it, insisting on it. He makes the insistence sound slightly menacing, but that's me, my interpretation. We kiss and part. It strikes me as strange. I wipe my mouth which has become a habit.

Paris remains bitterly cold. Over recent years February in London has been like spring. I wasn't prepared for this.

It keeps attempting to snow but doesn't quite material-
ize. I don't know whether it has snowed elsewhere in the
country. I suppose it is likely. I obviously take no notice
of the television. I only put it on as a challenge to see how
much I can comprehend. I'm improving with each new
day. Maybe that is another reason for delay, postponing
the important call, vanity, my need to do it right, gram-
matically speaking. I go down to Trinité, towards splen-
did Paris, a stone's throw away from Opera and Galeries
Lafayette, a normal world of expensive retail. I feel I am
doing something very strange indeed.

I go into a telephone booth. I read the instructions
three times. I take deep, difficult breaths. I can feel my
heart-beat thumping inside my chest. I am tempted to
walk out, go to the shops, lose myself, but resist. It is too
late for such minor indulgence. I am committed.

Finally I call the number. A high-pitched young woman's voice announces: "Allo, Médecin Sans Frontières."
I don't immediately reply. I expected to talk directly. I
feel flustered, all my carefully prepared phrases lost. She
impatiently repeats: "Allo, Médecin Sans Frontières."

Eventually I stammer: "Allo, est ce que je pourrais
parler à Dominique Dufour, s'il vous plait."

"Ne quittez pas. Je vous la passé."

I wait nervously, dizzy with concern, struggling against
the desire to break off, to abandon the mystery, leave it in
a phone booth in Trinité, and then she comes on the line:
"Allo, Dominique Dufour." Her voice is hushed, rather
husky, full of richness.

"Je m'appelle Madame Tennant, Louise Tennant."
There is a period of silence, silence in which my heart
floats, no longer beating but quite stilled. "Je suis la mere
de Joseph."

151

"Yes, hello Mrs Tennant." The sound of English calms, eases the tension. At least I will be able to talk.

"I was given your number."

"Yes, that is all right. Where are you?"

"I am in a phone booth in Trinité."

"You are here, à Paris?"

"Yes."

"I did not know."

"I was told that you would talk to me."

"Not now. Meet me for lunch. You are at Trinité. Let me think. Go to Madeleine and then Bastille. I am in Rue St Sabin. But don't come here. I will meet you in Bastille."

"But how? How will I know you?"

"Do not worry. I'll stand at the corner of Rue de la Roquette, outside the Metro. I have a pink and white coat, the pattern in squares. Say to me, excuse me but do you know Paris."

I repeat the words, my voice feeble, disbelieving: "Excuse me but do you know Paris?"

"Yes, good. And you have the street?"

"Yes, I think so."

"Tell me."

"Rue de la Roquette."

"It is a nice street. All right?"

"No wait."

"What?"

"When? You didn't say when."

"Sorry. Yes, of course. At one o'clock. At the corner. Don't be late."

The line goes dead, the termination abrupt. There is something fearful in that, something that causes a woman to forego formalities towards another woman. It implies a message that isn't ordinary. But I am seeing everything

152

second-hand, gradually being brought to the reality of something I am only seeing in a mirror at the moment. The reality terrifies me. How far from known things will this reality take me, my dead son, killed on continental soil. Is that what broke Frank into pieces, fear of the real thing. In his case that of a naked woman. He never seemed afraid of me, not in bed, beneath him, subject to him. He didn't complain about women, he complained about everything. But Frank was a drug head, his brains disconnected. And they would have me believe that of Joseph. Well I refuse it.

Perhaps I have never known him as I once fervently believed I did, but they can't make a complete stranger out of him. There was a bond, there was a commitment. I don't believe the story as it is constructed. There must be other reflections. I am ready to brave whatever Dominique Dufour has to say. The trouble is, looking at the time, I have three hours to wait. I don't want to stray too far. My directions are from Trinité. At that thought I almost burst into laughter. The idea is ridiculous. I know my destination. I will know it from anywhere. I know Paris. I head for the shops. After all, they are warm.

I arrive far too soon. Of course I had the injunction not to be late. It makes me wary of Dominique Dufour, the fact that she feels able to command me like a recruit; though with her husky, exquisite voice I can't really think that she will overpower me. My thoughts are running wild, my heart racing, my stomach churning, body and mind suffering together. I am absurdly early, thirty minutes to get through. Maybe I don't really know Paris, the time required, the distances that can be covered. I pride myself that I came here from Chausee d'Antin not Trinité which is a petty bit of vanity and entirely misplaced. I am learning too much about mother and son.

There is nothing for it but to wander around Place de la Bastille. John says that for him history began with two revolutions, one industrial and one political, the first thanks to a peruke maker from Compton, the second thanks to the release of seven bemused prisoners from the fortress here. He says the enjoyment of history is that it is possible to move freely between centuries seeing entire movements of thought, the constructions of religion, the nation state and empire, revolution and revision. He reads in it an endless struggle for freedom. He cares a great deal about freedom. I don't suppose he would be pleased by the freedom I have shown.

The sky has turned blue, the sunlight hard and brittle. The air is cold but bone dry. There is still some wind but it has no strength, though it remains sharp and biting. The sunshine makes Place de la Bastille seem larger. I feel less hemmed in. Naturally the Bastille is a symbol of release. It seems a worthy feeling to have prior to my meeting. I might actually have some courage, a residue of strength. I start to look for her, even though it is still early. For a second or two I think I see Bill across the square. It's absurd, of course, revealing my need for an ally, one that I shunned, a need I told myself was unwomanly. If he were here would I welcome him? It is too early to say. Whoever it was is gone in a flash. I stroll towards the corner of Rue de la Roquette. Five minutes ahead of schedule she appears, a woman in a very smart pink and white checked coat. Coming close to her I can see she is above medium height, has auburn hair brushed back from her forehead and hanging loosely around her ears. Her face is an attractive oval, her parted lips delicate, well defined. She has a roll-neck top, the collar braided and beneath it a string of gold. Dominique Dufour is a striking creature. I approach her, smile, and say: "Excuse me, but do you know Paris."

"Hello, Mrs Tennant, Joseph's mother, it is very good to meet you," she replies, her voice thick and contained. She looks around, and shivers a number of times as if the breeze were penetrating deeply into her. "Come, we'll have a drink and a sandwich, two friends meeting for lunch."

She turns and directs us down Rue de la Roquette. As we walk she asks about my stay in Paris, how long I have been here and what I have been doing. I lie, saying that I have been here a couple of days only and that I have taken in the sights. I make no mention of Bill. She wonders why I waited before contacting her. I reply that I was scared. She doesn't question that word at all, but rather purses her lips as if it were entirely understandable. The café she chooses is large and open, spread over two levels, five steps leading to the upper. There is music playing loudly. There are posters across one wall advertising forthcoming bands. The place is full of young people, students I suppose, given the bags, the files and the way they are. She tells me it is a safe place to talk. What am I to make of such a pronouncement? I smile. The gesture strikes me as ludicrous, but Dominique Dufour takes it as meaningful and returns it in kind.

"I was told that you would speak to me," I begin, having come this far wanting to hurry things, hear whatever she has to tell me about Joseph.

She smiles airily, raises her hand and wafts her fingers in front of her like a delicate basking fish, suggesting caution. At this moment the waitress comes to take our order.

155

Dominique takes charge, suggesting that a sandwich is probably enough, sandwiches and tea. I comply with everything. I have no appetite, no feeling in my body. "It's good to eat," she says, as if she knows my feeling, though she might mean something else entirely. I want to reply but can think of no suitable response. She waits until the waitress has gone away and then asks: "Who told you to speak to me?"

"I was told you would speak to me."

"But who?"

"I don't know. I thought it was someone called Amy, Amy Tomlin, but she said not."

She sighs quietly, her expression mildly downcast: "You see, that could be a concern or nothing. I don't know. That is always the problem, things which don't exist, things which do. I do not know the percentage. Is fear just a fragment or the most? And you Mrs Tennant, how do I know about you?"

I am surprised to be asked to prove myself. I can't immediately work out the enormity of that. I feel the stirrings of anger, but know that is misplaced. My loss, my grief, my being adrift, my being here, state everything. But I can't bring myself to blurt out such things, not because I have made them private, but that they seem threatened. I simply say: "I don't know."

"No, don't worry Mrs Tennant, I accept you."

"Can you tell me about Joseph?"

She shrugs and skews her face: "He was angry, an angry man, sometimes an angry boy. Sometimes it was like a little boy tantrum, and then grown-up, but you will know that."

I know that he had sad tantrums, outbursts of frustration when something was over. He had tantrums after

156

Christmas, because he hated it being over, Christmas and his birthday, the excitement, the pleasure. I shake my head. "What was he angry about?"

"His work."

"I know that he had lost his job."

"I don't know that he had lost his work, I think perhaps the work lost him."

"What do you mean?"

"Well, he was caught . . ." Just as she is beginning to explain herself the waitress brings our tea. Dominique asks for a pot of boiling water, and says to me that if she drinks tea it has to be very weak. The tea is for me. I tell her that I prefer weak tea too. Such trivia will either bind us or break us. The waitress goes again and Dominique picks up her thread. "I know he really wanted his work and I think believed in it very much. I think he was proud actually. And I would ask, why not? We should never let our concerns and scepticism blind us to the truth of things. His work was very good. I understood that to be the case. But the things he was asked to work on made him change."

"Change?" I ask, already feeling the weight of the word, its permutations of altered identity, a lost son, someone removed from me, becoming a vagrant exile. And I suppose that change has made me an internal exile, sentenced to my own confined wandering, caught in a world without substance, its realities glass.

"I mean he couldn't ignore some of the corrupt practices that went on. He wasn't able to continue. In the end he had to go. That was difficult for him."

"You mean he left his job voluntarily?"

"It is not the right word, but yes, of course. He came to us and said he could give details of research being

157

cancelled because the company thought it would threaten profit, and research being suppressed because it would damage the launch of a drug, damage the whole company."

"Research that Joseph was involved in?"

"Yes his research. At least to begin. At first he was in London and it was his research. He was looking at proteins in the brain and how they form plaques that lead to dementia."

"He was working on dementia?"

"Proteins, yes. Something to stop the protein developing in the first place."

I feel a great surge of sympathy and concern. Of course he would want to research the proteins and plaques of Alzheimer's disease. It was only natural. But does that reveal something of how he saw his grandfather, and then his father and himself in turn? I always play the game of continuing personality, disregarding anyone who suggests loss and bereavement. I get angry at the carers in the home for the facile way they jolly John's father along and take no account of his mind.

On one visit he told me that everything was white, the walls white, the floor white, the people white, even the bread white. There is a theory, a theory of love, that states that human beings need comfort, attachment, inclusion but also occupation. I'm sure he is dying of boredom. Of course I make out that his dementia words are next to mystical, but would I have him back, master again of his wooden sky-blue sea house, of course I would.

"Was his research successful?"

"No, no, I do not believe so. His research wouldn't do anything for those with the disease, so the company saw no profit in it. But the work on proteins revealed something else, something about the mechanism of autoimmune response, the way proteins triggered certain reactions at the neural synapse. Some work was instigated to look at the relief of pain in arthritis. Joseph was asked to work on that, but very quickly he started finding problems. When they managed to inhibit the autoimmune response they found small deposits building in the brain. They might have been nothing but they might have been something."

"But what did Joseph conclude?"

"He didn't. He was moved. He had to leave London. I don't know where he went after that. I was told, but I forget."

"Leeds."

"Yes, that is it. Leeds. I have no experience."

The waitress brings our sandwiches and pot of hot water. Dominique stops speaking. She immediately reaches for a sandwich and starts eating, only nodding her gratitude as the waitress departs. I find I have no appetite at all. We have ham and salami sandwiches. The thought of the salami almost makes me retch. I don't know why that should be. I have learnt nothing of Joseph that is taboo or disturbing. It is understandable that he hadn't told me what he was working on. He probably thought it impossible to tell me. I was always telling him his grandfather was just the same, going on about the beautiful things he said. It was obvious he would want to work on it, why wouldn't he?

Eventually Dominique dabs her mouth with a napkin and continues speaking: "I don't know what he was supposed to be working on in Leeds but he heard things from London, rumours, stories. Things were not quite right with the results."

"Who told him?"

Dominique smiles, eats another piece of sandwich, and then sips her tea before continuing. "The food here is very nice. You should eat something. I have no idea who told him. A colleague, a friend."

"Dr Tomlin."

Dominique raises her hand in objection. "If the person in question has not spoken to me I don't want to know."

"Why not? If research is producing adverse results then it is in everyone's interest to have that data known before . . . Well, before too much money is wasted for one thing, and before something terrible happens."

"Can you imagine the amounts of money involved, Mrs Tennant?"

"No, I can't."

"The figures are colossal. Something to address the pain of arthritis would take any company into the bracket of the very richest. They are not going to halt research on the evidence of a few speculative protein deposits."

"But these things would come to light. Research standards are rigorous. Joseph said things had to be tested and tested again, proven to work by others, open to peer review."

"I'll tell you how it works, Mrs Tennant. A new drug can make a company phenomenally rich and therefore also anyone involved in getting that drug to the market and off the shelves. A new drug creates a lot of noise, miracle cure, miracle drug, claims which the companies do nothing to dampen. The advertisers from the company tell a journal they'll give it say, $100,000, to run a special edition on the particular drug, plus they'll give the journal so much per reprint. The company suggests the so called best experts on the drug and also the editor for the edition. The company then contacts everyone who has ever said anything good about the product and invites them to fly first-class to, let us say, Madrid or Chicago to a symposium with the guarantee that their paper will be published in the special issue of the journal, so another publication for the c.v. After that the company can show doctors a digest of the work of the symposium.

"Remember, once a drug is produced the company hold a patent which means they are the only company that can produce that particular product effectively stifling any generic drug being made. The company will do anything in its power to extend patents and with the money to call on large corporate lawyers usually manage very effectively. When the prize is so great it follows that trial results are manufactured and negative results suppressed."

I can't place Joseph in this story. His scale is both smaller and greater, bound to the earth but possessed of vision. He believed in the idea of cure. If there was a wound he was sure it could be healed. He was driven by a simple creed, that his work was useful. And his rewards were big enough. I'm sure that was the case. He never aspired to first-class trips abroad. In many ways his impulses were the same as ours, John's and mine, to get close to something and peer at it, constructing meanings, making things. Dominique's world is too large. "Are you suggesting that Joseph manufactured research?" I ask, knowing that she isn't, but needing to ask because I'm the mother and I don't want any misunderstanding.

"No," she says, looking mildly startled, which is not a look I've seen. "No Mrs Tennant."

"No," I say, "I know. I just wanted to be sure. You said 'us'. You said Joseph came to us. Do you mean that he came to Médecins Sans Frontières? I know Médecins

Sans Frontières have campaigned against restrictive patents."

"Yes, Médecins Sans Frontières have campaigned against the practices of the big companies. But no, he didn't come to Médecin Sans Frontières. I am involved in a group called Reclaim. What we say is: reclaim water, air, seeds and genes; reclaim land and shelter, forest and ocean; reclaim health, education and humanity."

I gaze at her for a moment or two, this carefully dressed, affluent looking, exquisite woman and try to place her in the midst of those lofty ideals. At first there is a discrepancy between them, but slowly the things cohere. There is nothing in what she has said that I wouldn't want to stand for myself. I do wonder what it all means in reality though. For myself I have always known that awareness of things never meant particular political activism of any kind. I wear different ribbons throughout the year, awareness of this, that and the other, but it doesn't mean I do a single thing. "What sort of a group are you?"

She eats for a while, finishes her sandwich and then wipes her lips. She drinks her tea, again wiping her lips. Perhaps she is not going to answer me. Perhaps she is weary of saying what kind of a group it is. The majority do not belong to anything but majority groups and are cynical about others. Perhaps she is sick of cynicism and detects it in my question. Or perhaps she doesn't trust me, my understanding and my sympathy. She doesn't interpret the fact that I am jealous of anyone who can belong. I think belonging is a fine thing, a difficult thing, a wonderful thing.

Finally she puts down her napkin, having carefully folded it and pressed its edges between her fingers and says: "It is a group of people who come together, primarily on a website, who share similar aspirations and promote those ideas and whenever possible expose abuse. We have people from all over the globe doing just that, saying what is happening on the ground, bringing attention to the largely unreported issues affecting people every single day of their lives, our lives."

"And you?" I ask, wondering about her role, what she offers this group.

She inhales deeply as if fatigued. "I have been on six missions for Médecin Sans Frontières, but I am not as immediately available as I was, so now I arrange for other people to go on missions." There is a note of impatience and temper in her voice.

"Why are you not immediately available?"

"Because I am pregnant." She immediately falls silent and gazes at me long and hard, harshly perhaps, tired by my inadequate probing.

"You are a doctor?"

"No, I am a nurse," she replies flatly.

"I'm sorry," I say, then quickly and passionately correct myself, "not because of your news, being pregnant I mean, sorry that I have to wonder about the people Joseph went to. I am finding out about my son. I have been told that he abused drugs."

"No," she cuts in, "certainly not to my knowledge."

"I was told he had levels of drugs in his body. And alcohol."

"I have seen him drink wine. That is all."

"What happened?"

She shakes her head. The gesture doesn't convey lack of knowledge, but rather a suggestion that her knowledge is too difficult to say. "I don't know what happened," she says, her voice lowering. "The two of them said they

163

intended to go to Pont-de-Roche. Joseph knew someone there who wanted to talk."

"Wait, wait. The two of them? Pont-de-Roche?"

"Joseph and Joanne. Joanne. You don't know Joanne?" I shake my head. "Joanne is one of Reclaim. I don't know how they met, but they came together. I have known Joanne to talk to for many years. Joanne is very good. Joanne brought Joseph to my attention. She said he knew a great deal and wanted to tell others. It is a brave thing."

"They came together?"

"Yes, together."

"As a couple, as friends, as colleagues?"

"I said, they were together, a couple."

"Did they love each other?"

She smiles discreetly. "I am not the person to answer that. They had a flat together. I can tell you. You can try and talk to her."

"What did she say to you?"

"I haven't heard from Joanne. I presume she is keeping out of sight. I don't know whether she is still here or not. I really don't know."

"But you sound worried."

"Of course Mrs Tennant, I am very worried. I have to assume but I do not know. I allow myself to be optimistic but I do not know."

"What do you mean?"

"They say your son abused drugs and I say I have no such knowledge, so someone is lying. Does that clarify my worry?"

We both stop speaking. Suddenly I am aware of the music. It is mainly at the back of the café, where a large group of young people are gathered, spread around a number of tables. We are sitting to the other side, a table in the window. The street outside flows on in its repetitive way, people and vehicles, everyone making a living in the usual ways. It has never seemed more unreal. Everything seems unreal, and no longer to be trusted. I have been admitted to something that puts everything at risk. I could if I choose reject it all. Dominique knows that, knows the precarious nature of the existence of Reclaim, knows the ways its ideals can be swept away as facile and fantasy. Do I believe, sitting in this pleasant, boisterous café, that the safe comfortable world I occupy is capable of corruption and conspiracy? I would be crazy to think otherwise.

That admission brings Dominique and me into sharp focus, brings us together in the flesh, away from mirrors and reflections. For a while everything goes still which feels dangerous. A sound, a voice, a piece of music, a shout from the street breaks through and sends my pulse racing. The easiest thing would be to put some money on the table, thank Dominique for her company, and rejoin the life outside. But that is impossible. "And Pont-de-Roche?" I ask.

"There is a research centre there. The work was transferred from London. Joseph knew someone, someone who was concerned by the research that Joseph had already done and wanted to discuss it. Joseph thought he could get his work back."

"What do you mean, get it back?"

"When he left the company they confiscated all of his data, claimed it was their intellectual property."

"But it was his research, Joseph's. He had done all of the work. How could they confiscate it?"

"It was done in their laboratories, with their money.

They can always claim that the information is sensitive and of use to their competitors. This person also had information that trials had been conducted in the Ivory Coast. Drug trials conducted in the third world – the majority world – are cheap, easily set up and, more importantly in this case, have lax regulation. This is what brought Joseph to us initially. He thought it was the trials that would get our interest. Of course he was right. But we care about all of it. Of course, all of it."

"And now Joseph is dead."

Dominique doesn't respond. She looks uneasy. She obviously thinks that I am implicating her, her and the organization she is involved with, an organization of people sharing their experiences, exposing the smallness, bigness, grandeur and malaise of this poor suffering planet. Do I mean to implicate her? Of course I do, her and countless others too numerous to list. I blame everyone. I also blame me, and John. We have all failed, fallen short of the mark. I repeat it, to hear it for myself, not merely to create an effect. "And now Joseph is dead."

"Yes," Dominique confirms quietly, "Joseph is dead and I don't know what has happened to Joanne."

"You say they went together."

"They said they were going to consult with the Big Pharma."

"What does that mean?"

"Pharmaceuticals. The big pharmaceutical. They were going to challenge it. They were going to talk to the person inside, retrieve Joseph's data and build up their case. When they had the facts they would be able to use the Reclaim website. It might not shake the world, but that depended on the case."

"A joke, a pun, like a game."

"Yes, I suppose so, if that's how you would want to call it."

"No, it isn't how I would call it."

Dominique purses her lips and shakes her head. It is a mild gesture, yet charged with meaning. She doesn't minimize my loss. She recognizes it very well and multiplies it with the loss of the case Joseph was building, the wrong he wanted to right. She sees his loss for himself. She recreates someone with meaning and purpose, something the others – I don't know how else to describe them, enemy seems too dramatic – have tried to annul. I owe Dominique Dufour. She has returned my son to me, albeit a new one, one with terrible imperfections, but nevertheless him. I say the words: "Thank you." I utter them quietly, but with force. She doesn't know what to make of my gratitude or what to do with it. She simply shrugs, a throw-away gesture that wonders what good she has done at all. I ask: "Rennstadt, where is it from, who owns it?"

She smiles: "Rennstadt and companies like Rennstadt don't have nations, they are altogether bigger, that is why they are so powerful. They can pick up and go wherever they want. They bring billions into the economies of the minority – the developed – world. Who dares challenge that? Who dares put the case that they do not and cannot serve the real need of humanity? It is one of the great tragedies of the modern age."

"Can I have the address of where he was living?"

"Will you go there?"

"Unless you say I shouldn't."

"I think a grieving mother can go places that others might shy away from."

"I intend to go to the village."

167

"I will not tell you not to."

"I owe you."

"If you find Joanne, please, let me know. It is very easy to be scared but then they will have everything their own way. I would like to be less scared."

"I'm sorry."

"Who gave you my name, Mrs Tennant?" she asks, though it is not a question rather an illustration of hidden things.

"I am grateful to them."

"That is something at any rate. I really must return. I am interviewing candidates this afternoon. We have a number of missions that need volunteers."

"I'm sure your mission is very good."

"The cause?"

"Yes, the cause."

She writes something on a piece of paper, stands, says farewell and wishes me well, once again asking for any news regarding Joanne. I tell her that I will keep in touch. She pushes the paper across the table. As she steps away I pick it up. It is obviously the address I asked for. Shortly after, I see her in the street, hurriedly going on her way, not looking back once. The waitress comes to clear the table. I offer to pay but she tells me that the other lady has already done so. I am so grateful to Dominique Dufour.

Chapter Fourteen

The brittle, bright light of the afternoon is gone, replaced by a murky gathering of evening. There is a rush to vacate the city. I feel like an obstacle in their way. I have no direction, no destination, I am just here, caught in stasis. I have no choice but to be buffeted. At least the dry wind has cleaned the pavements. I will not return to the hotel feeling soiled. I am sick of being soiled. I am back in Trinité. How quickly it has become home. How quickly I have come to rely on its familiarity. It is pleasing to look into shop windows knowing that I recognize them. I like particularly the patisserie and chocolate shop on the corner of Rue St Lazare and Rue de la Roche Foucauld, though I do not have a particularly sweet tooth. Its display is so luxurious, indulgent and yet innocent. Or at least, I assume it innocent. But I suppose it wouldn't take a great deal of digging to reveal that chocolate and sweets are tainted. It is a world of spoiled pleasures.

I should have paid more mind to the familiar and the pleasurable. I always wanted Joseph to take on, be angry, stand up and be one of those counted. I wanted to be proud, my son the campaigner, the activist. I wanted him to argue and be concerned. I wanted him made in a certain fashion, fit for the challenge. And I never knew it, but he was. He was everything I wished for. Maybe it came late, I don't know, don't know anything really. I know I risked his death. I am at fault, guilty. My proxy parenting is disgraced. Why didn't I see that everything was well? He should have been in a laboratory producing improved washing powders, better whiteners, detergents called snowflakes in a world that was snow white and fairytale. He should never have taken on. He should never have listened to my abysmal schooling. I had something special and wished it away. He deserved parents with proper ambitions, wealth, goods and grandchildren, not some godforsaken idealistic dream. John and I are found wanting, our values, our spirit and our hope. I am a two times murderer fit for nothing. I am a two times murderer fit only for the rack.

Bill is waiting, eager for news. He has obviously been sitting watching the television with the owner. They have been drinking beer. He is at home, comfortable. For some reason I resent it, but find that a difficult feeling to comprehend. He wants to know what I have discovered. I tell him I have learnt nothing, nothing new, nothing worth knowing. He frowns at me, his expression doubtful and perplexed. But who was the girl, he wants to know. I tell him it was just a friend, not even a friend, an acquaintance, someone my son met on his strange wanderings, during his exile. Bill queries my last word. Whatever do I mean? I shrug and explain that my son was exiled from himself for a while, exiled from those things that he knew best, those things he cared about. He suggests that I seem to be saying that there is less mystery surrounding events than before. I ponder this, but can't commit either way. I gesture with my hand, implying a scales, balancing. He scowls good-naturedly and questions the fact that I have said I have learnt nothing. I don't reply.

I move away from him, heading for the lift, in my

170

mind leaving him to his beer and whatever talk they were having. He calls after me, asking me what time I want to eat. He isn't asking me whether I want to eat, whether I desire his company, or even anyone's company, simply what time. He is making an assumption, taking a liberty. My instinct is to say that I am not hungry, but then what will I do all night? I can't stay in my room, it's too dreary, too oppressive. Besides, I am hungry. I scarcely ate anything at lunch. I turn, put out my empty hands and tell him to decide. He says he'll knock at seven and returns to the television. As I enter the lift I can hear his laughter. He sounds like a man pleased with himself, and why not, he has made himself at home.

Once again we eat in Chartier. It is his choice. He thinks he is pleasing me. In fact he is condemning me. I am a betrayer, a cheat. My crimes are multiplying. I am a liar, a fornicator, an adulteress, a two times murderer. There is no hope for me. This was our restaurant, John's and mine, and I am destroying its memory. I will never be able to expunge Bill from it. I have failed entirely to preserve it. It is now just a place to eat. If I carry on like this I will flatten the known world, wipe away its landmarks. Part of me hates Bill. It grows with each passing moment, each word of concern and each offer of help. He is growing vulgar and lumpy in front of my very eyes. But it isn't his fault. He is not at fault. I am looking to make him the scapegoat for my wrong-doing. He is just being himself. I really do find his messages of concern and desire to help increasingly burdensome, though. I don't know where that stems from. I think I am maybe beyond help. There is something so obviously self-pitying in that thought that I refuse it. All I know is that I have made dinner a trial. I have crushed my own appetite and once again only manage to nibble at my food.

"You're not yourself tonight," he says, watching me lay down my fork and knife with a weary sigh.

"I'm just not hungry."

"Is that because of what you heard today?"

"I told you I didn't hear anything today."

"I don't actually believe you."

I glare at him, suddenly infuriated: "And what gives you the right to think anything of it."

"Because I care," he says, unabashed. "I find I care about you a lot. I also find that you seem more troubled with each passing day and that bothers me because at the same time I'm with you and I'd like the opportunity to help."

I look at him coldly, which seems something I can't control, and without undue force say: "But I don't want any help."

"I don't understand. Why are you shutting me out like this?"

"Because I can't cope with it." I am tempted to add that I don't feel I deserve any help, but that would open the demand for even more explanation. I just know that I have to confront this alone.

"Do you intend to still go to the village?"

"Yes."

"Then let me come."

I shake my head, without looking at him. I can sense his rage. I am not at all sure who is at fault here. He seems to think that sleeping with me means I have to be open to all of his whims, virtues and demands, whereas I admit to nothing but adultery. I say: "I don't ask to know anything of you."

172

"Then ask, ask whatever. I want you to know."

I shake my head again, this time lifting my eyes so that I can see him. His face is a static, staring mask, fixed to a single moral message. I can't deflect or defend myself against that. I remain silent. I have no questions to ask.

I say no to more wine, dessert or coffee. I suggest it would be better just to go. We return straight to the hotel. He leaves me inside my door. We are obviously not going to spend the night together. I'm not sure whose decision that was. There were certainly no words between us. The parting wasn't difficult but it wasn't easy either, perhaps clumsy best describes it.

It is only a quarter past nine. I'm not ready to chance the attempt to sleep, but can't sit in this deadly room. I go out, stroll up the road and go into a bar opposite The Blue Cat where I sit in a window so I can watch the life outside. At this time of night The Blue Cat is wide open, its daytime secrecy cast aside. A girl sits on a stool in the door-frame, her legs crossed, her bulging shapely thigh milky in the pale blue glow from within. Every so often another girl joins her and they talk and laugh. Together they call to passers-by. When they are together it seems like a game. When she is alone it is altogether a more hazardous and solitary life, perched on a stool, apparently fair game. Perhaps that is why I keep Bill at arm's length. I don't want this to be a game. It is real. I need it to be real. I am seeing the girl through glass, which would send Frank into madness, but her reality doesn't escape me. Selling sex to strangers, however much they are fleeced and cleaned out, is a terrible act of womanhood. In her borrowed space she is an object of infinite variety and meaning, staggeringly false in every one. I should be careful; I could go mad as well.

173

I drink a bottle of wine and then return to the hotel, suitably floating, ready to sleep, to have my usual dose of nightmares, an on the run murderess, a disgraced wife and mother.

Chapter Fifteen

Noisiel is a terrible disappointment. It is the suburb where Dominique Dufour says Joseph and Joanne were living. It is a chaotic place of concrete walkways, subways and steps. I was given directions at the station but very quickly have become hopelessly lost. There are rows of low storied flats, set in perimeters of green space. Every few yards there is another roundabout. The traffic is light. I feel as if I am behind the main routes in and out of the city. I didn't tell Bill I was coming today. I want to be here alone. In some ways I feel it is a macabre sight-seeing expedition. What really will I discover about Joseph in such a place? Already I have decided that the girl, Joanne, will not be here. I don't know where I think she is, simply fled, gone back to whatever is familiar and normal for her, her moment of adventure concluded. I left the hotel early, avoiding breakfast. I dashed past the open doorway of the breakfast room, fully expecting that Bill would call me back. Would I have stopped or rushed away? He didn't call, so the question is immaterial.

I acquire further directions from a group of elderly women standing together along the street, flats to every side. I don't know what they are doing. They don't seem to waiting for a bus but simply gathered, talking, wait-ing for a stranger like me whom they can guide. I hand over the piece of paper bearing the address. Should one of them crumple it up, wantonly destroy it, then my search will be over. I am reliant on good-will. There is some discussion about the best route to take, by road or through the flats. Eventually they agree on the latter. Their directions are easy to understand. My skill is returning. I am again becoming a competent French speaker. It has taken longer than usual. I am getting old. The evidence multiplies. Am I still capable of new thought, new insight, or am I only able to live out discoveries I have already made? I wonder what my counsellor would say to my being in Noisiel. Am I moving on or digging in deeper and deeper, all movement constricted and closed for the foreseeable future? But there are varied emotions at play here, grief and detection, together combining to make something new and rather incomprehensible. Where is this leading me? I fear the worst.

Once again I feel that I am lost. There are flats all around, set in the middle of neatly cut swards edged with pavements. It is rudimentary, the outline of a possible place rather than a real lived place. There are no people to be seen. A lower ground flat to the left has its windows wide open, with music sounding out, not blaring but loud. A young man appears and leans out. I traipse across the grass and again ask to be directed. He is impeccably polite, which surprises me. It is deplorable that I am surprised, but I can't deny it. He draws me a small diagram with arrows taking me through a sequence of concrete alleys. He reassures me that I am nearly there. My gratitude is real, if excessive. Within minutes I have found what I came for.

The block in which Joseph lived is a large rectangular complex with numerous entry doors. There are long rows of wide concrete steps leading up to it from what is presumably a parking area but today holds a market, a bustling, crammed market. Alongside the door I want are two cash tills. There is a group of black youths leaning against the walls, blocking the doorway. We stand looking at each other for a while, one in particular eyeing me with a fixed yet languid stare. It troubles me. I apologize but say I need to get to the door. With slow, mannered movements they make a space for me. In looking at me, what do they see? Would I recognize that image if it was shown to me? And if I didn't would it mean it wasn't true? I suppose seeing is everything, images subjective.

Joseph teased me about seeing. He said that colour is a myth, something we see only because we have the rods and cones in our eyes to allow it. Colour is imposed on the world, he said, and all creatures see the world differently, constructing it according to need. He smiled at me, his flamboyant artist mother, as he explained that the need a human being had was to be able to pick out a red apple from a green background. Of course, he was inferring that such primitive need formed the origins of art. I don't suppose he wanted to rubbish my material, just assert his knowing, his own particular seeing.

I push open the door and find the stairway to the upper flats. Joseph and Joanne's was number five.

I knock repeatedly, three raps followed by a period of silence. With each attempt the sound deepens and the silence deepens, the two becoming internalised. What am I trying to do, summons my dead child, draw him back from his false death to his true destiny, indulging myself in the perverted magic of hopeless hope? This is not my child's home, not a place he should ever have called home. A home is a subtly created space, a space of negotiations, agreements, mutual identities. This is a shelter. But perhaps that is what Joseph needed, a refuge

177

from hostilities. I knock again, a final drum beat, a final grieving call. The door of the adjacent flat opens and a young woman appears. She is tall and thin with olive skin, her expression listless. She doesn't speak but simply gazes at me, or even past me, her interest in me being purely mechanical, the person making the noise.

I explain that I was hoping to see the people who live here. She looks confused, perplexed. Perhaps she knows that one of the people who lived here is dead and doesn't want the responsibility of breaking that news. Eventually she tells me that no one has been here for weeks. Does she know what happened to the people who lived here? She shrugs, but I can't read whether that means she doesn't know or isn't telling. How were they, I ask, the question slipping involuntarily from my mind. From a complete stranger I want a good report of my son, confirmation that his actions were worthwhile, meaningful.

All she can say is that she didn't have any trouble with them. Her starting point is the expectation of trouble. It seems meagre. She goes on to say that it is much quieter now and she has little children, so she doesn't miss them because it is quieter. I look at her questioningly. Still without animation she says that there were people coming and going all of the time, doors opening, closing, banging. Sometimes there were rows. She supposes the couple had rows but says it isn't any of her business, everyone has rows, just she didn't like the fact it was next door because she has little children. She qualifies it by saying they sleep through anything and yet still she isn't sorry that the flat is quiet. She supposes they were involved in drugs, everyone who has visitors at all times is involved in drugs. She says it isn't any of her business but she has little children and she doesn't want them mixed

178

up in anything like that, though she doesn't doubt they will. She is already crippled with defeat. I shake my head and say that I don't think they were involved with drugs.

She smiles for the first time and tells me she knows these flats, knows just what goes on here. I tell her that sometimes there is a gulf between appearance and reality. She asks if I am with the other people who came. I tell her that I'm not and that I know nothing of any other people. She shrugs and says they were here for a while, looking around. I ask her how they got in. She has a key. She can let me in if I want. I say that I do want, though I don't suppose I really do.

The flat is a mess, the floor strewn with clothes, magazines, drinks cartons, food wrappings. Drawers hang out, their contents draped over the side. There is a smell of dampness and mould. The windows have been covered with old sheets pinned into place. The entire place is chaotic. I turn and ask the woman if the people who came did this. She shrugs and an incomplete smile crosses her lips. She doesn't know that it wasn't always like this. I can't accept what she has suggested. Surely Joseph couldn't have lived like this. I try to recall whether he was a tidy person or not. It seems such a simple piece of motherly knowledge, but I don't know. I kept his room in order, and Sara took over. When he was at university he shared lodgings and couldn't be responsible for how they were. I simply can't say. But this has to be more than normal disorganization. These rooms have been ransacked. Why am I always allowing doubts into my understanding of Joseph and trust myself so little? I insist on it. Joseph was a well-ordered, organized person who could not have lived like this.

I ask the woman if she knows anything about the girl.

179

She just shrugs. When was the last time she saw her? She has no idea but it was a while ago. She hasn't seen anybody but the people who came and me. I move through all of the rooms, each as messy, jumbled and disorganized as the last. The kitchen is squalid, the sink mouldy, the walls black, surfaces smeared with grease. The whole place is squalid. I try to visualize Joseph here, try to hear his voice, place him, but it is impossible. I cannot equate Joseph with this mess in any way. I am beginning to feel sick. I can't begin to think what I have learnt here. In pursuit of his purpose was Joseph willing to put up with squalor? Or had the girl Joanne brought him to this?

I call to the woman and ask to know what the two were like. She counters by questioning why it is I don't know. I step back into the first room where she is waiting, picking my way around the rubbish, and tell her I know one very well, the boy, that he is my son, but no, I don't know the girl. I am aware that I have said that the boy is my son and not was. She doesn't have to deal with that. She looks sorry for me and then pleased with herself. She tells me that the girl was pretty, but nothing more. I have to make do with Joseph's aesthetic discernment.

I thank her and tell her I have seen enough. We obviously both feel we should say something on parting, perhaps that we'll meet again when they return, but we both know that is a lie. In the end I turn away and make towards the stairs. She calls me back and asks whether it will be all right to lease the flat. I ask her who owns it. She shrugs and tells me the landlord of course. I turn and leave without answering. It is not in my gift to dispose of the wreck of my son's shelter.

Back at the hotel I ask whether Bill has returned. I feel foolish because I don't know his surname. The man at reception knows exactly who I mean and tells me that he has left, checked out that morning. He looks at me sympathetically and with some apology adds that there is no message. I smile and say I didn't expect one. I have what I apparently wanted, to be alone, to cope alone. I say that I too will be leaving in the morning.

On my last night in Paris I eat once again in Chartier, claiming it back, telling myself that I can do it. The trouble is I find that I miss Bill, miss his concern, his formidable singularity, his straight ways, whereas I should be missing John. I betray again and again. Afterwards I drink in the bar opposite The Blue Cat. This is all mine, my memory, my exclusive space. I end up quite drunk but I am not bothered by anyone, and can't decide whether that is something with which to be pleased or disappointed. I betray everything.

Chapter Sixteen

The village of Pont-de-Roche is situated a few kilometres from Orleans on the Orleans canal. A guide-book would describe it as a charming, typical French village with scattered farmsteads with red tiled roofs, set amidst rich agricultural land and forest. It is just the sort of place where John and I would stay. A village with a bakery and a greengrocer, places to walk – woodland and canal towpaths would be perfect – yet close to a reasonable size city because on holiday we like to eat out, a chance to order local cuisine and dress up. We like to dress up, go out smart, make an effort. We do it for each other, proof that it matters how we look in each other's eyes.

I don't know why we lost the urge to travel. I suppose like a lot of people we became a bit sceptical over the years. It came with an understanding that the world is no longer to be discovered but defended. The tiny, ill-used planet is being overrun with western tourists who couldn't care less about local people or local customs and don't pay a penny into local economies. We could never accept being a part of that club, not willingly, so we made a stand, no flights, no packages, no trampling on exotic soil. It doesn't really explain why we stopped visiting the old haunts we always had. It all got wrapped up together somehow. We went to the Lake District often enough and loved that. Were our thoughts so high-minded and correct? I think so, but I am a little forgetful. We maybe just became set in our ways. And now John has gone to America. He clearly has fled. I must have driven him insane.

There are large hoardings at the fringes of the village advertising all manner of things: furniture, carpets, restaurants, supermarkets, hypermarkets. They are part of the landscape. I used to thrill to the sight of French hoardings and road-signs – the priority signs, route signs and place names, particularly Paris passing through Abbeville. They were an announcement of difference and promise of delight. The sign posts of Pont-de-Roche suggest no such thing. They signify unguarded remarks, acts of omission, heartless interpretations. They tell me that I have been an insufficient mother; that I have failed. They point to the destination of my son. He died here. This is the worst place on earth. My love of this country has turned sour. My love has proved sham. My love was an empty thing. My love is mammoth.

It is late afternoon. The sky is fiery crimson, the cloud scattered and fragmented suggesting myriad shapes. The eye can construct anything; mine opts for figures, incomplete figures pulling themselves from a restraining background, like figures emerging from flames, from iron-ore, from clay. I would challenge the notion that I am summoning the dead. I don't have that strength. I simply can't escape earth beings, try as I might. They circle me like sentinels, austere, magnificently formed guards, but are they watching me in order to help me or hinder me. I presume the latter. I feel desperately alone here. I am so close to Joseph and yet the closeness also tells me just how far away I really am. It is a closeness that destroys everything. The sky with all of its multiple shades is a tent over nothing.

I have rented a small cottage outside the village boundary, set some way back from the road. I saw the sign for it from the taxi I took from Orleans station. Having sped past I asked the taxi driver to go back. In my mind I think I realized that I couldn't stay actually in the village. The woman who owned the cottage said she never let it out before Easter. I didn't think she was going to relent. She informed me there was a hotel in the village, at the cross-road. She turned away from me suggesting that the subject was closed. I blurted out that I was the mother of the boy who was killed here. That changed everything. Of course I could stay. She had already begun airing the rooms, preparing for the new season. She did wonder whether I wouldn't be more comfortable in the hotel. I shook my head. I didn't have to explain a need for space, a need for privacy, the shake of the head was enough. I thank her greatly. She gave a quick explanation of the layout of the area and left me. I haven't seen her since. She is obviously leaving me to mourn.

From the cottage the quickest and easiest route to the village is along the canal towpath. The canal is wide and long, its waters murky, the colour of milky tea. The towpath is rough and pockmarked, pitted with puddles and patches of mud. My small boots will be ruined. It seems such a derelict thought to consider my footwear, even momentarily, but the mundane batters at my head to be let in. I mourn my boots. It was a pleasure buying and wearing them, and now in Pont-de-Roche they are wasted. In the quickly gathering twilight there are swift flashes of blue, the dirty water broken, circles lisping to the bank. I presume they are kingfishers but they are too quick to really see, particularly in the failing light. Before long I can hear traffic ahead. Each individual vehicle is an event, the sound at first distant, becoming louder and louder until it passes and the sound fades, becoming distant again.

Eventually I reach the road. It crosses the canal and is accessible by a path running up to it. The lights of cars send search-beams into the night-sky. I ascend to the road and stand to the side. There is no pavement and the road narrows as it joins the bridge. There is a steady, but broken, passage of vehicles. Each one sets my nerves on edge. I can hear the sound of collision. It is buried deep within me, inescapable. Of course I have no idea of the precise location where Joseph was hit, but it was here somewhere. I suppose I'm searching it out, looking for its hideous sign, wanting to capture it in the same ghastly colours as it was then, with the night thick all around, the roads night-time busy. I know the woman at the cottage could have told me, but it's better that I see first, have an image in my mind. I am constructing reality here, turning the invention of Pont-de-Roche into something drastically real.

I turn right and go into the village. In no time at all I reach the cross-road. It seems that everything of note in the village is at the cross-road: a handful of shops, a bar, a restaurant and the hotel. The shops are closed, the shutters down. The cross-road is something of a dilemma. Where do I go? There are too many choices, too little information, no knowing. I turn and flee, back across the bridge and heading into darkness. I wonder if this is the bridge that gives the village its name. I suppose it could be old enough. In my mind I had the image of an ancient white brick, hump-back construction, fit for horses and carts. Of course it would have no place in the modern transport system. Maybe there is such a bridge; maybe

185

all kinds of hidden things will be made visible before my time is out.

I don't know how far I walk, but it seems like miles. In the dark, with the traffic passing in both directions it might seem farther than it really is. I know distance deceives, and deception is an easy thing to latch onto. As the last vestige of crimson disappears from the sky the traffic becomes increasingly sporadic, until it is eventually intermittent. At the same time the temperature drops. It is not as cold as it was in Paris; in fact the mid-afternoon was noticeably warm, suggesting spring, an early spring of mild frost, crispness and cleanness. After a while there are virtually no streetlamps anymore, and stars appear in the cloud breaks. The moon is a thin, narrow sliver, its further shape resonant but unseen. I resent the suggestion of beauty. There is no beauty in this place, only horror, only catastrophe. Its outlines have been stained, events embedded in its tissues, its name soiled. As always since I have been here I cannot distinguish between a desire to scream, cry or vomit. Perhaps I am moved to all three.

I keep going. At a point where the road bends there is a track running away to the right. In the distance there are lights and I can hear the sound of engines running. Without thinking too much of it I make my way in that direction. The track is rough, with potholes difficult to see in the meagre light. To either side are tall but bare hedgerows with a drainage ditch running alongside, the occasional glug of seeping water discernible. As I get closer I can see two lorries parked side by side, their engines droning, loud in the still night air. The track must lead to a patch of waste-ground. I stand, watch and listen. There are a number of voices, raised voices but not arguing, rather debating, making plans. Moments later

186

I hear the sound of footsteps crunching on the rough ground behind me. I turn quickly. I am confronted by the figure of an enormous man, only his large blacked-out outline visible. He stops immediately. We are both evidently trying to decipher each other in the dark. It is impossible. He comes on, his step slow, menacingly so. I consider running, shouting out for the men at the lorries, but do nothing, simply stand, passive and numb.

He comes up close, stands over me and leans slightly towards me, almost as if he wants to sniff me. He is wearing a large black jacket with the collar turned up, his hands firmly in his pockets, his great bulky shape hunched forward. I feel that I'm going to be engulfed and crushed by him. I look up. His face is close to mine. It is a large, square shaped face, with high cheek bones, leaving defined hollows running down to a broad well shaped jaw, the skin thick and finely fissured. He raises his eyebrows and slightly pouts his lips, and his eyes light on me with interest and pleasure. I quail under his attention, it seems so direct and personal. He reaches for me. I feel a scream rising in my throat, but it won't issue.

He lays his hand on my right shoulder and speaks to me quietly, his voice guttural but with a musical lilt, and which surprises me, in hesitant English: "Over there, to right, the canal. It goes with the road. Under the bridge and then with the road. To the other side, the big pool, the water thick, bad smelling. In summer you would be eaten by insects. A little farther the . . . – how is it – *scierie*, yes, sawmill. And over there the laboratories. It does not have a placard but the company is Rennstadt. And so, what interest have you?"

I shake my head, slowly, with difficulty. I can't think. I don't know what to do. Again the feeling of screaming,

187

crying or vomiting assails me. I am collapsing in my own well of absurdity, perplexed by the identity of things. No matter how hard I try I can't summon my voice. He smiles grimly and shakes his head.

"I think you should leave the lorries. They are very busy. I can see it. Too busy for anything. Do you understand?" I manage to nod my head. Again he smiles grimly, and again shakes his head, but rather in the fashion of a disapproving parent. I feel small and ridiculous, devoid of purpose. I resent the fact that he makes me feel this way, but I can't resist. He imposes his scale on me. It is a brutal, masculine power. "Good," he adds, by way of conclusion I suppose. There is a period of silence, the two of us not moving, not responding. Eventually I step away, circle around him and slowly walk away from him, walk away as if he is sleeping and I am escaping. I go no more than a few feet when he calls: "You can find the way?"

I nod, but quickly realize that he won't be able to see that. "Yes," I say. "I will find my way all right."

"It is dark now."

"I know but the road is straight."

"The cars they go very fast. Be careful."

"Thank you, I will."

There is nothing else said. I edge away. I look back once or twice and he seems still to be there, standing in the same place, not having moved at all, but it could be a trick of the dark. At most his presence creates a greater depth to the darkness, but it could simply be that I am looking, imagining him still there, imagining him altogether.

I go straight back to the cottage. Despite not eating since lunch I have no appetite. Luckily I have brought wine. There are two bottles in my suitcase. I open one, slump down on the settee and put on the television. There is a programme in English with French subtitles, an American police story of some kind. I kick off my boots in order to put up my feet – my ruined boots. I can't help but feel it is undeniably disappointing. Real life is a puzzle. The programme ends. That is disappointing too. I have no idea what it was about. I switch it off and simply sip at the wine. I don't know how long it takes me to finish the bottle, but not long. I don't open the other. I will need a clear head. I am grieving, not drowning.

Chapter Seventeen

The police are sympathetic but not helpful. I have been ushered into an office and offered tea or coffee. I don't know the position or rank of the policeman assigned to talk to me, he doesn't say. I presume he has been chosen because his English is reasonable. I don't suppose they are chosen for their skills with the bereaved. It is not their job to assuage the human consequences of a crime. They have to take a realistic view, work within simple parameters of right and wrong. As he keeps telling me he can only say what the report says. He keeps saying it without actually telling me what the report does say. Of course he is uncomfortable. He won't be able to trust to my response. Perhaps I will start wailing and screaming, and what will he do then?

"All right," I say, trying to imbue some sense of being in control into my voice, which is a lie, an act, "tell me about the official report."

He stares at me for a moment as if needing to digest my request. He has very sharp, birdlike features, with dark penetrating eyes. I feel their investigative intensity. They seem to be asking – what is the point of such knowing? What good will it do to know the criminal facts? In this case the victim is dead and nothing is going to change that. I nod at him as if he has actually presented me with a question. He shrugs and opens the file in front of him. When he talks it is from memory, the file a prop, a symbol of officialdom.

"I do not know what I can say, Mrs Tennant, more than there was a terrible accident."

"How was it an accident?"

He looks concerned, as if the explanation requested is too complex, too absurd, too much a product of grief. "Your son was hit by passing vehicles. He was run over three times."

"I know, I know that. That is the information that was relayed to me in London. What I am asking is how you know it was the collision with a car, or whatever, that killed him?"

"But what else, Mrs Tennant?"

"That is what I am asking," I say, my voice rising in intensity, not shrill but deep, enriched. "Have you investigated all of the possibilities?"

He looks annoyed, his skill questioned. He visibly stiffens and sits back in his chair, preparatory to speech. "I can assure you Mrs Tennant that the French officers did everything they should. English officers would not have done anything differently, I am certain of that."

I lower my head, downcast. I have been misunderstood. This is not about chauvinism of any kind. I am being cast in the wrong light. "No," I utter quietly, penitent for his sake, "I am in no way suggesting that. It's just that I was told that my son had drugs in his body."

"Yes, Mrs Tennant," he replies flatly, as if his case is proven, as if my affront has been rebuffed, "that, unfortunately, was certainly the case."

"But how?" He eyes me quizzically, needing some explanation of my implication. "Yes, how?" I go on. "My son never used drugs."

He visibly relaxes, feeling certain, I am sure, that he understands the situation, the denying, grieving mother,

191

the refusal to face disturbing truths. There is another surge of sympathy from him. He may even tell me about his own children. "Mrs Tennant, it must be difficult for you. You must ask yourself how well you know your own son."

"Very well."

"But grown-up, not before. We lose sight of our children I think."

"My son had no use for drugs."

He shrugs, raising and lowering his eyebrows quickly, mildly bemused, knowing he can't win this pointless argument. For him it doesn't matter. He has his file. But his file is wrong. This has to matter. "I think Mrs Tennant, it is understandable."

"What drugs?"

"Excuse me."

"Name the drugs in his body."

He leafs through the file, pauses at a certain page and then gazes at me with an expression of deliberate concern. We have no need to do this, he is suggesting. We can leave it as it is, mysterious, a sequence of hints, guesses and suppositions. I nod, giving my permission, asserting my need. "Well," he begins speculatively. "the toxicology report states that there was evidence of opioid, diamorphine di-acetylmorphine, which you probably know is heroin. There were also other unknown chemicals."

"Unknown?"

"Not individually, but because they had metabolised, not known in the original compound."

"My son had no use for drugs."

He eyes me impatiently, obviously satisfied that he has given me more information than is reasonable. "Mrs Tennant, your son was a chemist, known to produce his own products. Unfortunately it has led to a terrible tragedy."

"Who told you that?"

"In the course of our inquiries we learnt that your son had lost his position in his company because of his behaviour. There is enough evidence to believe that your son used drugs he had himself manufactured."

"Who told you?"

"I cannot name people, Mrs Tennant."

"The company say it. The company are the keepers of my son's identity. The company construct him to suit their purpose. The company make it the way they want. This is absurd and wrong. How can it be? What are they protecting? And we all see what we are told to see. It isn't surprising people go mad. Maybe I am, maybe I really am, and that wouldn't be surprising, would it. But it would suit people. So no, I am not mad."

"Mrs Tennant!"

"I'm sorry; my voice was shrill, I know."

"There was also alcohol present in your son's body."

"Yes, so I believe. I have seen him drink wine. He certainly liked wine, French wine. He would have been happy here, but never a drinker, not even when he was a student."

"But how can you say with certainty, Mrs Tennant?"

"I am sick of being told that I don't know my son. I have done him that injustice too many times. I have betrayed him over and over again, but I think I need to stop." He shrugs, unable to respond. "Do you intend to continue your investigation?" I demand.

He looks perplexed. "Everything is complete. All reports have been made. There is nothing more to consider. It is over, Mrs Tennant. I am sorry. I cannot tell you what you want to hear, I know that."

"No, I'm sure you can't." He shrugs again, knowing that this impasse cannot be resolved. He will have judged me in some light, possibly favourably for my loyalty, symbol of my love, unfavourably for my naiveté, my refusal to believe in the visible world. He will resent that refusal, that going against the grain, but I have seen what mirrors achieve. I understand that at least. I am about to be dismissed. I am not finished though. How could I be? I present my final petition. "Can I see the place where it happened?"

He considers for a moment, probably weighing up available resources and then firmly states: "Of course, Mrs Tennant. Do you want to go now?" I nod, confirming my intention. "Then I will take you myself."

I half expect to cross the bridge again, but we don't. The bridge is the first turning to the left after the police station and we go straight on. This road is the larger of the two. This is obviously the main route somewhere. Not a major route, but not insignificant either. In no time at all he indicates and pulls over. We are on a stretch of straight road, forest to the left, open fields to the right. There is a single horse in the field, standing still like a carving, dappled grey, its belly round. Its head is over the fence, but it makes no move at all. I'm sure it would make an inadequate witness. I walk along beside the police officer, cars, vans and trucks speeding past, the chill air moved. He stops and looks down at the roadside and says: "This is the place, Mrs Tennant."

I feel an instantaneous sensation of choking. There is no discernible change in the ground, no memorial, no object or symbol marking the spot. My mind rushes, panicking, demanding certainties. How can he possibly know? He could just be saying it to finish with me, to be done with it all. But I have to know. I will have to carry this for the rest of my life. The significance of it is too great to comprehend. I look at him, my expression pleading, needing confirmation. I gesture towards the faceless ground, my entire self seeping away in horror and uncertainty. "Here," I say, my voice scarcely audible, my attention fixed to a miniscule patch of the earth's surface.

"This is where his body was discovered."

"But died here?"

"Yes, our inquiries would suggest that is the case. His injuries were not those of a big impact. He fell, too much drug and alcohol, and unfortunately in the dark he was run over three times."

I am crying uncontrollably. It is such an ugly place to die. It has no shape or definition. How could he die here, marooned, on some meaningless roadside? "But why here?" I plead, speaking through the emotional outburst. "Why would he be here?"

"Unfortunately he is the only person who can tell us that."

"It is good that you say so much is unfortunate."

He looks mildly embarrassed. He says: "I mean what I say."

"I know." I walk on a little way, surveying everything, fixing it in my mind. I know that in no time at all I'll begin to lose sections of it. I won't quite recall the view in the far distance, though I will insist on my accuracy. I need space and time. I don't know how human beings survive their grief. It seems to burn and destroy so deeply I can't visualize any recovery at all. I go still farther and then panic that I am leaving the true place behind. I scan everything once again.

On the crest of the hill I can see the figure of a man, a

large, straight-backed shape. I'm pretty sure it is the man from the previous night. He inserts himself into my grief with a jolt. Why should he be following me here, here of all places? I sense danger and I am not so lost in grief not to be aware of it. It feels like yet another betrayal. I return to the police officer. I suggest that I'll walk back, wanting more time than he can possibly allow. He refuses, suggesting that the road is too busy to trust to a distraught mother. I argue only so far. In the end I agree to return with him. I don't mention the man on the crest of the hill. He was too far away for me to be certain, besides which I wouldn't be believed.

As we get back into his car I ask: "Why could he not have been drugged, sedated, and then brought here, dumped?"

"Because it didn't happen like that."

"There is a piece of music goes over and over in my head."

He shrugs. I don't pursue it.

I walk out of the police station without my soul. I don't know another way to describe it. My inner being has been cored out, left to gape like a horrified mouth. Nothing has colour, savour or value. Everything has died in this dreadful village.

Chapter Eighteen

I have no idea how long I have wandered or where I have been. I have been dealing with the problem of my son. He is large and potent but unavailable. I can't comprehend that absence. His image in my mind isn't clear and yet he is part of everything I see, the fields, the forest, the canal and unfortunately, as the policeman would say, the road. It will always be the case. But it should never have been. He could have had a completely different life, one that was quietly anonymous, stay-at-home. The age offered it. He didn't have to go to war, take on foul ideologies or stand for a cause. It is the age of capitalism triumphant, the end of history. He didn't have to fight it. But he did. He found it wanting and he fought it. It is wanting. It destroys life.

I suppose it was inevitable that I should find myself here, at the gates of the subsidiary of Rennstadt which, as the big man suggested, has no name-plate, no billboard. I don't really know what I intend to do – confront them with their hideous crimes, list their abuses, shame them, tear down their walls, or just present myself, their victim, a passive symbol of their worthless practice.

I step into a small, relatively dismal reception area. I approach the desk and ask to speak to someone in authority. The receptionist asks me what my business is in connection with. I reply that it is in connection with a life. She shrugs, pouts her lips into a beautiful whorl and turns away. She whispers into her telephone and then suggests I take a seat. There is a single chair against the opposite wall. I sit and wait. Five minutes later a door alongside the reception desk opens and Bill appears. He looks directly at me, a moment of recognition crossing his face, and then he says something to the receptionist and approaches me.

He stands over me, looking down, something of the nature of a smile on his lips. He speaks airily, charging his voice with deliberate friendship: "Mrs Tennant, always a pleasure. And how is your husband, Mrs Tennant?"

I can't work out whether he knows anything about John or not, or whether he is fishing, warning me off with the threat of exposure. "My husband is very well," I say.

"That is good. He is too busy to travel with you, I suspect."

"He has a lot on his plate at the moment."

Bill smiles. "I assumed that to be the case. I wonder if he approves of your being here."

"Of course."

"Approves of everything you do, I suppose."

"No, unfortunately, not everything."

"That is disappointing. I wonder if he approves of your making wild, groundless accusations against this company."

"He supports me in every step."

"Is that so, because I wouldn't want him to get into trouble on your account."

"Trouble?"

"Oh yes, Mrs Tennant, trouble, legal trouble. You see I have been instructed to inform you that if you make any more malicious statements about this company you will be sued."

"I will expose your crime."

"Dear me, my crime. I think we were in that together. You were a little bit pious for my liking, though with quite a tongue I seem to recall."

"You're nothing but a bastard."

He comes close and utters in my ear: "We are tired of your antics, bothering our staff, turning up on our doorstep. You are the mother of a drop-out drug-addict, now get used to it." He stands back to his full height. He smiles: "I don't think there is anything to add, is there. No, well, goodbye Mrs Tennant, it was all very, what's the word, bland."

I can feel an irresistible, shapeless pain. It is satisfying in some way. I still feel. I have not been emptied of all humanity. I feel my soul resurgent, resisting, defying this act of destruction. It refuses to accept that this is the stuff of human beings. We have not degenerated to this extreme. My pain is exquisite. It is composed of good things. I smile at him. I say: "Thank you. Thank you, you have given me something back." He looks sceptical, his monstrous uncertainty bubbling to the surface. "At least I know that you are really quite worried by me, why else indulge yourself like this. I won't stop, not now, not ever."

He frowns at me. "You shouldn't say such things. It isn't helpful."

He turns away and begins to walk off. Against my better judgement I call to him: "And is your wife all right?"

He turns back, smiling: "It's a shame actually, but you just missed her, though I don't think you would have got on, scarcely anything in common."

"Perhaps we will meet though."

199

He scratches his neck with his index and middle fingers, smiles and says: "No, you won't, you really won't."

I regret asking. It serves me nothing. I need to escape such things. My strength is in freeing myself. Somehow I am surviving. It must have purpose. I have to give it purpose. I am guilty of bringing up my son to need to stand for what is right. I can't betray him ever again. There is a tune inside my head. I am reminded of its beauty. I exit wanting to do justice to its notes.

Chapter Nineteen

Back in the cottage I take a shower, cleansing and reviving myself. Encounters with people leave me soiled and weary. I don't know my place with them. When I took the train here I was struck forcibly by that separation. I kept seeing my reflection in the glass and wondered about myself as if I were another person. What does she share with all the other people on the train, I thought, with all of the people on the other side of the glass, on platforms, in the fields, in the streets. What does she share with all the people whose time she shares: they intersect, but what does that mean? Is there a purpose to this accidental gathering and sharing that she can't see? I have to be more concrete, more alert. It isn't she, but me. The reflection was absent more than it was there, and there was only me then, sitting, wondering, unable to turn my mind to anything useful like reading. Maybe I'm just not looking. Looking, the critical interest on top of the experiential interest, will bring something into existence, but will it be real, or will it be a sequence of notes seen in interconnecting mirrors. I don't know anything anymore. Everything is a mystery.

There is a spotlight directly above me. When I look down I can see the shadow of the cascading water along the floor of the bathtub – the shower is above the taps. The shadow is slow and heavy, as if the water were falling in slow motion. The reality and its capture don't agree.

The shadow is beautiful and compelling. I feel like weeping it is so exquisite. Once I would have accepted without question that moments of beauty can result in tears, but now it seems unfortunate in the extreme. When I turn off the water the silence and stillness are surprising. My response is somewhat predictable. I intend to drink until the exquisiteness of all things is not in doubt, though its truth may be painful in the extreme. At least I make the effort to dress, lying to myself that I intend to go out and eat.

I don't know how much later it is when the sound of a car rouses me. Two thirds of a bottle is gone. I'm sure I haven't slept but I seem to have been dawdling through story dreams, crazy dreams of hide and seek in which I didn't really know whether I was looking or escaping. I presume it's the woman who lives across the way. The cottage isn't attached but is like a small outbuilding. I go to the window and look out. I can't see anything but I hear a car door close. It isn't slammed but firmly pushed to. A few seconds later another door opens and is pushed to in the same deliberate, discreet manner. I pull the curtain behind my head to stop the light from the room in order to better see through the dark. Along the track, just at the point where it divides, turning into the courtyard of the house or straight on to the cottage, I can make out the front part of a car. Its sidelights are still on. As I look the full lights are switched on illuminating the whole area in front of the cottage. It is like an assault, disturbing the peace. There is usually a lone horse in the field on the other side of the hedge and I wonder what it would make of such sudden, artificial light. I suppose it is stabled in the evening. The night is cold, though the day had a moment of spring. There are snowdrops on the path to the canal, a great swathe of white, tenacious and wonderful. Somehow I have drifted from the present to flowers. I worry about my mind. I am so scattered and leaking.

The headlights are switched off. The dark plunges back, solid and physical. It shocks me into the present. I press my face against the glass straining to see who is there. Against the hedgerow, on the fringe between track and verge, there is a figure, the outline just discernible against the background. Scale and shape suggest a man. His head is tilted slightly back, suggestive of the fact that he doesn't wish to be seen, though the idea is absurd. His right arm is raised from his side, the open palm facing backwards keeping something or someone back. He moves forward slowly, step by step, keeping to the fringe. I jump back from the window. What on earth is going on?

I stand in the middle of the room, my hands clasped together in a stupid parody of prayer, paralysed. My first thought is to hide, but hide where? The cottage has no hidden corners, certainly none I know of. I'm not aware that there is a cellar or a loft. And even if there were wouldn't that just mean that I'd be trapped? But trapped by whom? Why do I think they are intruders? Am I not being ridiculous, interpreting headlights and slow steps in some maddening melodramatic way of my own? Why not go to the door and ask them what they want? Of course there must be more than two, the two doors, the driver still sitting at the wheel, lighting a pathway, controlling the dark. Surely this can't be happening. Terrible cries of torment and panic well up inside me, but I just stand and shiver. I feel that I might vomit. I fight against myself, shouting inside my head that I am being ridiculous, more than stupid. I am in rural France for God's sake, grounded in a predictable reality, not an actor in a hidden narrative. A much louder voice says my son died here. That statement demands no embellishment.

With the thought of Joseph two things occur simultaneously: my panic subsides, allowing a wave of fatalistic resolve to pass through me, and the door at the rear of the cottage opens. There are a number of rooms to the rear of the cottage: a small kitchen, a shower-room, a toilet and a tiny lumber-room. The door is between the shower-room and toilet. Of course I never gave a thought to it being locked or open. It has possibly never been locked since I arrived. I make no attempt to move. I suppose I have a martyr's pomposity. A few seconds later and the enormous man who placed his hand on my shoulder along the track where the lorries were, who appeared at the scene where Joseph was found, stands in the doorway. He looks at me with a quietly puzzled expression, almost as if I disappoint him. I urge myself to scream at him, wanting to muster all of the defiance of which my wretched little body and soul is capable. I want to say I am capable of fighting, but with that thought it all eludes me. I am capable of fighting for what? I have no such mission.

"You must come with me," he says, his tone low and commanding, its guttural musical quality as strong as on the night with the lorries. I make no reply, but gaze at him unflinchingly. "Quickly," he insists, his voice suddenly rising, but then continuing more evenly. "Trust me. You must trust me."

I virtually laugh in his face. That's what Bill said, trust me, on the first night we ate out, trust me. I don't suppose his name is really Bill. Of course I don't trust this man. I don't suppose I will trust anyone ever again, even though I need to. The thought releases all of my pent up fear.

204

The paralysis, the stupidity, the denial have all gone. Yes, this is happening. I am caught up in something, brought to it through the criminal death of my beautiful, gifted son. I will fight and resist all the while. I fix him with a withering look of triumph. He steps up to me, quickly seizes my arm and drags me away. At the rear door he lifts my coat off its hook and throws it over his arm, eases the door open slowly, peeks through the gap then pulls it wide and steps out bringing me behind. I know this is my opportunity. If I scream I should arouse the lady in the house, if she is there. As I'm thinking it through he drapes the coat over my shoulders and leaves his arm there, covering me, containing me, urging me to keep close. He bustles me away from the cottage towards the house, looking all around as he goes. The house and cottage are separated by a small wooden fence, the two connected by a gate. There are lights on in the upper rooms. If I scream and shout now she will surely hear me, but there is the evidence of the coat. He thought of my comfort. It was a spontaneous gesture. He just knew I needed a coat. Or is it to make everything look natural? A woman found without a coat would be suspicious, even one stricken with grief at the loss of her son. That will be the story. A mother visits the scene of the death of her son and overcome with grief takes her own life. I will be another fictional character in this story of mirrors.

He leads me through the gate then bends to my ear and utters: "Please, quickly, it is the good chance." His breath is warm on my face and visible in the semi-light, a small plume of whiteness, quickly displaced. "We must, quick." There is much concern and puzzlement in his voice. Of course I don't trust him, but I have to; I have no choice.

205

We quickly skirt around to the rear of the house, the house and cottage standing at right angles to each other, the rear of the cottage facing the side of the house. We follow a path through the garden and then at the bottom scale a small wall and then turn right to the house and run, following a hedgerow edging a field. When this hedgerow is intersected by another we turn and make towards the canal. Only when we reach the canal do we stop running.

A thin sliver of moon appears between broken clouds. The water of the canal is visible, a steady blackness, intimating depth and quiet. It is the quietness that is reassuring. Things may fall out in a pattern that is recognizable. I am beginning to learn that if you look you can bring something into existence. It is perhaps better that I avoid the canal. I want nothing from it but commonplace stillness. I look into the face of the man. He is no longer holding me. His release ushered in cold, a feeling of aloneness. I hate the momentary comfort I felt crossing the fields, running together. It was impossible not to trust him when we were running, we were so obviously conjoined, but the separation set that aside. Besides I have no need to trust a man. I hate myself for falling for that. Only John ever earned that right. The man is smiling, the tenor of it pleased, perhaps pleased at me. He says: "I am the Big Farmer, Le Grand Fermier."

I recall Dominique Dufour's words that they were going to consult the Big Pharma, Joseph and Joanne. "It was you they meant. They were going to consult you."

The smile broadens, the large, bone dense contours sculpting into warmth. "She calls me the Big Farmer, the correct big farmer. That is what she says. I like it." He throws up his hands and shrugs: "I am a farmer and yes, I am big." He laughs, guttural notes like bubbles.

"What did they consult you about? Do you know where the girl went?"

"Later, later, not now. Now we still go quickly." He takes hold of my hand, his touch this time more hesitant, self-conscious. I realize that his touch was always gentle. I remove my hand from his, put my coat on properly and then take it again. We head-off along the towpath.

After a few minutes I stop him, like a child pulling at an adult's hand. "What would they have done?"

He looks down at me, purses his lips and then says: "Whatever they needed."

"Are they French?"

He shrugs: "Not in doing what they do. Maybe, maybe not. It is not of significance."

"So what does it mean to them?"

"Money. Everything means money. It is a clinically simple, elegant decision. Please, to come."

"Yes, of course, of course I'll come."

Chapter Twenty

I lie in bed suspended in some mid-point between sleep and waking. My mind is a canvas. There are numerous small tears penetrating its surface, sequences of dashes, lines cut with zigzag serrated scissors, closely huddled smudges. Shapes come and go, constructing and deconstructing, turning fluid, losing substance. There is birdsong, lots of birdsong. I have forgotten the volume birdsong can produce. I have been turning the sounds into shapes, each shape a separate species. I open my eyes. Spindles of grey light illuminate the room. I am in the house of the Big Farmer, whose name is Pierre-Yves Moreau. I know nothing more about the people at the cottage. He told me his name, offered me cheese, bread and wine, which I accepted, and was told not to ask any questions. We spoke of other things, village life, London, John and his work in America – I had no reluctance disclosing my run-away husband. Pierre-Yves Moreau is a widower with three children. We shared a great deal, but nothing of the things that brought us together. There is pleasure, sadness and puzzlement in his face all at the same time. His features are bold, primordial and beautiful. I trust him completely. If I am mistaken – which, of course, I might be – then human kind is twisted and duplicitous– which, of course it is. I want to trust Pierre-Yves Moreau, it stems loneliness.

The bedroom is very comfortable, though scant. There

is a huge piece of dark furniture covering the wall to the left of the bed, with carved decorative lines and enormous drawers. The wood is so dark it is almost black. There is a chair in the corner with two towels. There are three paintings on the walls, all seascapes, originals in oil, impressionistic in style, verging on the abstract. I like them, like them in an easy, uncritical, joyful way. The sheets on the bed are pure cotton, cool to touch, perfectly smooth, smelling of cleanness. I haven't felt so comfortable for a long time.

I get up, push my hand through my hair, and dress in the gown that Pierre-Yves Moreau has also provided. To the right of the bedroom is a bathroom. It is obviously a man's bathroom, devoid of any clutter. I rinse my face and straighten my hair. I gaze at myself for a short while, debating whether this remains the person that so recently left London. Maybe more time has passed than I recall. It was winter when I left but this morning the birds seemed to be signifying spring. It has yet to snow, though it threatened so often in Paris. Perhaps that is how it eventually will die out, by failing steps. Perhaps that is how everything eventually dies out, one thing at a time, by fits and starts, with false dawns and sad endings. Yes, Louise Tennant remains tied to all that is Louise Tennant, all the moments of taboo and shame, a single narrative cemented by memory. I am an artist of motherhood, displaying imitation and allegory. I also aspire to the second theory of beauty and the third of idealised nature. I leave the mirror with foreboding and excitement. Just before retiring Pierre-Yves Moreau said that I would meet Joanne.

There is no clutter whatsoever in the house of Pierre-Yves Moreau, which is not to say that there is no comfort.

The sitting room has a settee and two chairs, high-backed with floral patterns, with plain differently coloured scatter-cushions. There is a small table on which there is an unfinished jigsaw, an extremely difficult jigsaw with hundreds of tiny pieces, the picture one of sea and sky. Pierre-Yves Moreau has obviously discovered a more benign form of preoccupation than wine. I should perhaps learn from him, though I do not have the temperament or inclination to solve jigsaw puzzles. Looking at the unfinished puzzle I am vividly reminded of something that, in the early years of our marriage, John used to say whenever he was asked about his work: *A thousand sad and baffling riddles.* He told me it was a quotation from a Liberal politician from the beginning of the twentieth century. I miss John, miss him so much. I feel that everything is a sad and baffling riddle. I don't suppose I will find any answer either.

The sitting room leads on to a dining room. There is a large pine dining table tucked beneath a window looking out onto a sloping garden. Besides the table and four chairs there is a sideboard, again of pine and very simple, with a single decorative bloom on each of the door panels. A door to the left leads to a small galley kitchen, again meticulously tidy. Pierre-Yves Moreau is making coffee. He asks me if I have slept well, which I am surprised to say I have. He smiles, looking genuinely pleased to hear it. He offers me coffee and croissants. I accept with real pleasure. I comment on how nice I find his house. He tells me that the farm has a larger house and that this used to be rented out as holiday accommodation, but since the death of his wife he has preferred to stay here. He laughs and says he now rents out the big house and gets more money which makes him feel worse. I suggest that there are a thousand sad and baffling riddles. He shrugs, perhaps failing to understand the English. I don't know how to say either baffling or riddles in French and don't feel that a thousand-fold sadness is a sensible thing to say.

We sit down together to breakfast. The garden has numerous empty beds, and clusters of bushes and shrubs. It falls away to a substantial orchard. The birdsong has diminished since earlier. The day is dry and bright, promising spring.

Having taken a few bites of croissant and sipped some coffee I ask: "What is your interest in Rennstadt?"

"They poisoned the water. The lake in the forest. The big lake. It is an old crime, an accident they said. They paid a fine, something for each dead fish, each dead thing, but it was not an accident. It was what? Laziness, lack of regard, vandalism. After that I watch and find that pollution is just how this company is, and this is the one I know. The world is full of companies, such companies. I don't use chemicals. It is how it is intended."

"You watch?"

He smiles. "I know that is not a great thing."

"No, I didn't mean that, not at all. I'm seeing you, seeing you watching, and maybe I'm hoping, and hoping isn't the right word but I have no idea what is, that you will tell me something about Joseph." A shadow passes across his expression and he looks at me with his usual sadness and puzzlement. He shakes his head, but I can't tell whether he is refusing me or making a comment on my behalf. "But you watch," I go on, my voice more shrill. "You said, so you saw something. I saw you at the place. I saw you on the hill."

He skews his face, perhaps embarrassed. "From the

211

time I know you are here, when I saw you near the trucks, I decide to watch for you."

I smile at his embarrassment, his clumsy way of saying he wanted to look out for me, keep me safe, a stranger, a grieving mother.

"But how could you know who I was?"

"In your face I can see it. It is there."

"I don't cover my loss with any skill."

"No, not the loss. Not just the loss. I see him and I know." I look at him sceptically, disbelieving. He smiles: "But yes, of course, you have that look, his look, purpose, work to do. He was like that, like you. I think very much of him."

How will I ever be able to thank Pierre-Yves Moreau for those words? At last someone has said something good about my beautiful boy. At the same time they burn me for the witch I am. If I had never burdened him with task and work he might never have come here. Why couldn't he stay in his estate house in Leeds, a good father and husband, enjoying the privileges of inactivity? Why fight such a big fight against such a big opponent? I know his response, the smile, the condescending grin and the nervous superiority. He did it because it had to be done. He was instructed in the possibility of right and wrong, and the certainty of grey areas. We educated him as we thought right. We never strove for outrageous things, just a good society encompassing all people. We never wanted to overthrow everything – though maybe John does, and tries to explain it to me – just make it better, make it right. Yes, reclaim water, air, seeds and genes; reclaim land and shelter, forest and ocean; reclaim health, education and humanity. We just wanted the answers to a thousand sad and baffling riddles.

I remember Joseph used to scoff at my ribbon days, all of my solidarity ribbons. I thought he was being childishly cynical, but now, knowing that he has the same face as me, I know that he knew it never amounted to activism. I never told him that I knew that as well, it was just that I believed in awareness too. Unfortunately, Joseph and I have so much to say to each other. Could any death be called good because everything had been said? There is no end of saying. I have much to tell John, so much to hear. I have been such a neglectful wife. "Thank you," I tell Pierre-Yves Moreau. "Thank you."

Again a shadow crosses his features. Of course he knows the magnitude of loss. He can't even continue living in the same house, though nor could he entirely abandon it. It is next door, his old life, his old self. Maybe it is a burden, this cement of memory binding us together into a single entire being, but how could we survive without it? Everything brings into existence its opposite. My pain is my joy. I have loved as a mother does, without calculation, desire or need of reward. I have known absolute love, known its scale of difficulty, its destructive lash. I need to say something to Pierre-Yves Moreau, something about what he and I both know. He must suspect something of the like because he speaks up, deflecting it, laughing with tense deliberation: "It was good you appear because I had minds to deal with them."

A sudden chill passes through me. The words of Pierre-Yves Moreau stop me dead. I can see John's father banging his fists in his room, calling out over and over again, I thought, I thought, I thought. Of course it was the wrong word. He was saying, I mind, I mind, I mind. The poor man was perfectly aware of his situation, of the walls closing around him at all turns, and no one to advocate

213

on his behalf. I mind too. I smile at Pierre-Yves Moreau and ask: "What were they doing that night?"

"I have seen them dispose of effluent into the lake and the canal. The fish in the lake have no eggs. They say everything is clean now, the problems solved, but it is not the case. At least here there are laws, people to stand up, make these things stop, but they will just go. They will devastate everything, leave poison sumps and toxic wells just to make money, but money for what, for the sake of money. The world has three tribes, the ones destroying, the ones trying to stop them and the ones who have their heads in the sand. Unless the second tribe is successful then it is all over." He shrugs and smiles: "Maybe there are always good things, I don't know."

There is something beautifully wistful about Pierre-Yves Moreau. He is a man of scale in all respects. I have no doubts about my trust. My only doubt would be failing him.

"You suggested that I will see Joanne."

"Of course you will see Joanne. She is in the house, but she comes here," he replies, his voice lowering. Evidently he doesn't even like going back into the house. Maybe that is because it has another woman, Joanne, whoever she is. I must admit to a certain trepidation at meeting this woman. My son abandoned his wife and child to be with her. She signifies him, his final choices.

"When will I see her?"

He looks at his watch, and then looks at me, his great sculpted features appearing austere, his passion withheld. He recognizes the difficulty in all things. He nods. His voice comes from a very low register. "She will be here soon. I said at nine, but she is not a perfect time keeper."

"No," I say, "I don't suppose she is." I have no idea why I should say such a thing.

Chapter Twenty-One

Joanne is surprising. She is small, slim and striking, younger than I expected. She sets up contrasts of black and white. Her hair is black, raven black, down to her shoulders, her face pale, the skin porcelain white, her eyes dark, her features small but perfectly shaped. She has a black jacket, white top, black skirt and black boots, big boots like hiking boots. She strikes me as both fragile and fierce. I am aware that I am studying her, taking in details – small details like the black mascara, the pink lip-gloss – without having spoken a single word. Of course the process of looking is a quick one, mother quick and artist quick, discriminatory. What does it say about her that she uses time to put on make-up? Does it mean that her grief is a minor grief, that her relationship with my son is not the one I have imagined? But, of course, the inquiring mother would also usually have her carefully applied make-up. We do things by custom and habit; I at least should concede her that. But in reality I am conceding her nothing, nothing other than that the woman in the Paris suburb was right and she is pretty, very pretty; given a different script she could be as pretty as a little angel, but I am being deliberately sardonic. I can't escape the fact that this is the person for whom my son abandoned his wife and child. There can be nothing right in that.

"I was told you had rows," I say, my voice flat.

She screws up her face, her torso stiffening. She is still

standing, framed by the kitchen door. "What?" she says, incredulous and annoyed.

"A neighbour of yours in Paris said she heard rows. She thought you had rows. I just wondered, that's all."

She eyes me fiercely, and then snaps: "Sometimes yes, sometimes real shouting matches."

"She was worried that you'd wake her kids, but they never did. Parents worry about things like that though."

"Are you for real? Have you come all this way to tell me off?"

"I don't know."

"Well, we don't have anything to say to each other." She looks towards Pierre-Yves Moreau and gives him a flustered frown of farewell. I catch his response. He seems dejected and disappointed. Yes, I have come all of this way to be disappointing. I think I stand by my right to be disappointing. My son died here, and this girl is in on it, instigator and partaker. They had rows. She pushed him, drove him to this reckoning.

"What were your rows about?" I call, my tone demanding that she remain and see this thing through. She looks enraged and embarrassed. I wonder on whose account she is. "I just want to know, my son and you. I just need to know," I continue, underlining the word need, the need that goes into saying it.

"I don't know what you want."

I catch her eye and in an instant let her see the scale of that need, the scale of distress that leads to clumsy openings, disordered questions, raw anger. "I just want my son. I lost him," I say, my voice dogged, unsentimental. "I've come to find him." She frowns, listening carefully, possibly concerned for my sanity. "I used to know him very well. I never knew he had rows in a Parisian suburb."

"The flat was a mess, a pigsty, and sometimes it got to us, one or the other. But it wasn't ours to clean up. It was borrowed, just a meeting place, but we had to live in it. So we rowed sometimes, each wanting the other to be the cleaner, but neither of us was that."

"So what are you?"

Again her eyes flash towards Pierre-Yves Moreau, perturbed and infuriated by me. I just keep looking at her. I don't want to see his disappointment, don't want to face it. She throws up her arms: "I'm a chemist, if that matters."

"You look so young."

"So? Look, and I'm only saying this because you're his mother and I feel for you, sometimes we rowed about tactics. Joseph wanted to publish material before we could substantiate anything. That would have been a disaster. We could easily have been discredited and then nothing we later said would have any credence. He used to get incensed by it all, just wanted to take it all on." She pauses for a moment and a small smile forms on her pink glossed lips. "He was passionate, you'll know that."

I shrug. Do I know that? Do I know anything of the forces that drove him, what his sense of justice and injustice was, his versions of right and wrong? I know what I wanted, what I trusted in, what I felt was right as a parent and wanted him to aspire to, but do I really know how it all turned out? No, I don't know anything. "Yes," I say, "he was always passionate."

She turns to Pierre-Yves Moreau again and holds up her hands as if surrendering something, and then addresses her next comments to him: "But we hardly ever rowed. I'm being made to say all of the wrong things. It's not how it was."

217

"Then how was it?" I demand, my voice shrill and impoverished.

"It was lovely if you want to know."

"Of course I want to know."

"It was special. We really had something, something special."

"He had a wife and child."

"I know that."

"Does it mean nothing?"

Again she looks towards Pierre-Yves Moreau, wanting to know whether she has any obligation to respond to my probing. She turns back to me and fixes me with a look that is both tolerant and defiant and then quietly says: "If someone has to be hurt why should it be the two people who love each other?"

"You loved each other?" She just stares at me, refusing to enlarge, refusing to face that love in these circumstances, in this company. She is right of course. I have no rights to be admitted to the details of their love. I have been denouncing it, calling it invalid. "But he had a child," I say, speaking to myself as much as her. She simply shakes her head, her eyes closing briefly. "It can't be right leaving your own daughter."

She repeats the same gesture, a simple, uncertain negative. "I've got nothing else to say."

"No," I say, "I understand."

For a third time she shakes her head, her eyes closing but this time with a minor explosion of breath, perhaps denying me, perhaps denying herself.

Pierre-Yves Moreau speaks up, telling Joanne to sit down. She has been standing throughout our exchange. I made her stand, as if she'd come to the headmistress' office. I should be ashamed, but I can't feel that. Pierre-Yves

218

Moreau stands and says he'll get more coffee, leaving his seat for Joanne. We will face each other across this great pine table, presumably with Pierre-Yves Moreau between us, protecting us, which he no doubt has accepted is his role.

We sit opposite each other at the same eye level, casting glances at each other, after which we turn to the window pretending to study the dormant garden. The sun is higher, the day brighter, the sky a pale springtime blue. Birds flit to and fro continuously. There is a bird-table and numerous feeders. The widower must still find that he has a mind for nature. At the moment everything seems such an absurd comedy to me, nothing worth anything. My son gave up his life for the girl opposite me. She is pretty, a flawed angel, mildly eccentric, testy and truculent – which is justifiable, given my treatment of her. I am struck by the similarities between us, her scale, her sense of style – which is not mine, but we both have one, deliberate and distinctive – and our love of the same man. I have not congratulated her on that but condemned her. I parade my loss as if it outdoes hers. There is something vulgar about allowing loss to become competitive but I think I have become vulgar. Grief has made me common and commonplace, my love of all that was beautiful absent. I could still expound the theory of line, chiaroscuro and colour but it is a sterile knowing. I could quote Klee saying it is the *realities of art which help lift life out of its mediocrity*, but that is lost with my loss.

I am adrift in this cottage, devoid of connections, making senseless assertions, abysmal statements, feeling abused by the reality of the figure opposite me. I need the unseen and the seen, the personal and the public, the past and the future to come together and form a coherent whole, which they never will. I am abandoned to my own mental wanderings, tortured by the insubstantiality of reality. What is the purpose of birth and death if it is to be measured solely by the time between?

I look directly at Joanne, trying to be calm and measured. "Are you still working?" I ask.

She looks at me, understandably suspicious. "As a chemist in a laboratory, or someone continuing the work we set out to do."

"Either, I suppose."

"Yes, I am still working."

"I find that I can't. I can't find any motivation."

"I find I need occupation."

"Yes, occupation is important."

"I find it so."

"It comes with the human need to be loved."

"Well, I don't know about that."

"That is the theory anyway."

"Which theory is that?"

I smile. "A theory about love."

"I feel close to him when I'm working, because it was his work too. They can't destroy that, can they?"

"Have they not?"

"I don't think so. If I thought that then they would have won. I would have let them, and I refuse to give in like that."

"And have they not won?"

"Not if we expose what he wanted exposed."

"Which is?"

"The truth."

"And after the truth?"

"After?"

"Yes, after the truth what comes then?"

"I'm not naïve. I'm a scientist. After this truth there will be other lies to expose, truths to tell. It will go on and on. What we do in our lifetime might seem very small indeed. But we do something. We do something useful."

"Was dying useful?"

"No, of course not."

"But that's what happened."

"The second crime doesn't make the first any less. We have to make a stand or we will have no dignity at all."

"It's a mission then?"

She shakes her head again, her eyes closing on me, but quickly opening. "I don't know what word I would use."

"A good mission probably."

"Maybe. But maybe I'd just call it an occupation."

"Full circle, of course. So did Joseph die for his occupation?"

"Joseph didn't die for anything. Joseph was killed."

"Do you really believe that? Do you really believe that such a thing could happen in a sophisticated, civilized country as this? Is it not fanciful, a bit simple?"

She looks at me intently, our level eyes engaging each other, no longer resistant. "If you look at the sophistication and the civilization for long enough, you'll see it's all made up, just a sham."

"A mirror within a mirror?"

"Yes, if you like."

"But knowing that leads to insanity. I've seen it, the resultant madness, the derangement, the thousand sad and baffling riddles."

"We all have to be vigilant, stand up against domination in all of its forms. The search for any truth is not a clear path to freedom. We have to be wary and a little bit courageous, though as for myself, I'm only so-so."

221

"You're very philosophical."

"Which is always portrayed in a poor light."

"No, not for me. I am married to a philosopher. My husband has an astonishing mind. Was it courageous taking his own drug?"

She eyes me with a look of sudden concern. "Joseph never took his own drug, he was given it."

Pierre-Yves Moreau comes back to the table carrying a pot of coffee. He has obviously afforded us time, listened as best he could to what was said and assumed we were in the process of making common ground. Is he right? He probably is. I am drawn to her. She has made me need her. I want to be admitted to her world of occupation, her understanding of love.

Pierre-Yves Moreau sits between us and pours the coffee. We sit together in silence for some time, shifting easily from contemplation of each other to contemplation of the garden. It seems we are as much out there, our thoughts engaging with the rules and laws of nature, the curiosities of the given world, and our means of knowing them, as we are in here, in this former holiday home. She is right of course, the act of looking brings things into existence, looking makes secret visions visible. Reality is a construction, a composition, formed and deformed, and formed again. We stagger under its rules, trying to free ourselves of things that are inescapable. She is quite right, we need our occupation. I need to move on.

"Tell me about Joseph's death. Tell me how my son died."

She flashes a quick look at Pierre-Yves Moreau, but she is comfortable with this. It is a moment of particular, measurable truth. She speaks slowly, quietly, clearly describing images inside her head, the fixed account of a terrible event. Will memory sustain it, or will it change, alter into a new story. It is hers, hers to do with as her mind dictates. For now I dread it, yet welcome it.

"We had only been here a few days, staying in the house, Pierre-Yves', when Joseph received a message, a text from someone asking to meet with him. I told him to ignore it." She pauses and looks directly at me. I can't tell whether she is asserting a notion of innocence or guilt in her failure to insist on it. Perhaps it is both. She still struggles with these things. I share so much with her already. "I should have been more forceful."

I smile, surprisingly, and say: "You had a row."

She laughs, gazing at me gratefully: "Yes, I suppose we had a row. We had no idea who the message came from. As far as we knew only Pierre-Yves and one person inside knew we were coming."

"Who? Who knew?" Her eyes flash at me suspiciously, wary of my wanting to know. Her trust has been damaged beyond recall. She is, of course, right to question my need to know. It comes from the same abuse of trust. "I'm sorry, I didn't mean for you to break a confidence."

"No, it's all right," she says, thinking it through, going over it again in her own mind. "Someone I had spoken to through the website often. And Joseph had met her, once, once only on a visit to the laboratories in London. They hadn't spoken a great deal then, but they knew of each other. I have no doubts over her. Really, I don't." She looks quickly towards Pierre-Yves Moreau, needing his corroboration, his agreement on trust.

He smiles and shrugs: "I do not know the person. It is better I do not, that she does not know me." He waves the idea away.

Joanne looks lost, the responsibility she has in the

223

narrative hurting her. "Joseph said that we had to take any information we could, that falsified trial data was just the tip of the iceberg. He knew there was so much going on inside, behind the corporate gloss – the illegal extension of patents through legal loopholes and governmental bribes, research on drugs to protect tourists while locals die, drugs for manufactured illnesses, preying on the paranoia of people's lifestyles. I can still hear him, Mrs Tennant, sad, angry, obsessed."

"Louise, please."

"I knew it was dangerous."

"Yes, I know."

"When Pierre-Yves found him he was raving." I flash a quick look towards him but he makes no acknowledgement of his part in the story. "He said he had come through a long white tunnel into a cleansed world. He said he could speak in tongues and had seen the purity take place. He thought there were no features or details to anything, that they had all been cleaned away. But he knew himself, sensed himself inside the white world. All life is sacred, he said." She pauses and looks at me questioningly, tormented by the hurt she is giving us both. "He wanted to be forgiven for ever thinking otherwise. I didn't understand. I don't."

I am sacred, comfot me, that terrible message erupts in my mind, but I stay composed and ask: "And you put this down to the drug he was working on?"

"Not at the time. Later when the toxicology report pointed to it. I knew they had given it to him. Joseph didn't have access to Nivis, how could he?"

"They called the drug Nivis?"

She smiles: "Because it was still being developed, a white powder like snow, so it was called snow. Nivis."

"But you can't know for sure that they gave it to him."

She skews her face. "That was the data they suppressed, that even in small doses it could cause psychotic like symptoms in people. But that wasn't the real problem. If the psychosis was minimal and very selective, maybe that's a price that it could be argued worth paying for such a drug, but Joseph found that in animal tests it was forming rudimentary plaques in the brain tissue, so the likelihood of long term cognitive dysfunction was a very real likelihood."

"Dementia?"

"Yes, I suppose, something like dementia."

She stops speaking. Perhaps I am supposed to say something, take my part in this narrative, judge it, give approbation to my heroic child. In the end he wanted to be forgiven. I find it sad and baffling. Had he struggled so much with the man his grandfather became, worried that the same fate awaited John and him? John thought he was intolerant, maybe even petty minded, despite the upbringing, the education. I just thought he was put out by the inconvenience, the sick man indoors, the human spillage, the sloppy eating, the poverty of words. I never ventured into the hardness for Joseph. I am at fault. I let them down, father and son, let them fall out, no longer seeing eye to eye. And at the last is that what Joseph saw, the perfection of John's father, the surviving soul of the man who in his sky-blue sea house taught him so much about love. I sigh deeply. Silence is my answer to all of this, the only answer I have. But Joanne is in limbo, in need of dialogue, in need of occupation. I smile weakly and say: "I never knew that Joseph experimented on animals. He obviously thought it better not to let me know."

"You mean that's what he wanted to be forgiven over?"

I continue to smile in my weak, shambling way: "Maybe, who knows. He sent me an email. I am sacred, comfort me."

Joanne purses her lips, downcast, hurt again by a fragment of the narrative new to her. Discoveries beyond our consciousness seem so large and harsh. I have not afforded her the ambiguity of the last two words. *I am sacred, comfot me.* When I say it aloud comfort me seems right; besides it is also a component of love. I suppose I can never be sure of any of it. Maybe he was scared and sacred. He was sacred to me. He is sacred to me. That is the only truth I need.

"I didn't think he was capable of sending an email. He must have done it when I left him alone, before he took off." She looks embarrassed. I wonder whether that is because of her lack of judgement or because he contacted his mother. We each have things to live with. I hope it draws us together, I am sick of being set apart.

"Took off?" I query, needing to know everything.

Pierre-Yves brought him in and we tried to get him to sleep. It took a while but I thought we had settled him. He was still muttering but it seemed like he was going to sleep. Pierre-Yves stayed a little longer and then left us. I don't know how much later it was but he started raving again. I went to get Pierre-Yves but when we got back he was gone."

"Why didn't you get a doctor in the first place?"

"Because I made a mistake."

"And he was hit wandering on the road."

"No, no he wasn't. He was dumped on the road later. They killed him."

"But we can never know that."

"I don't have to look very hard, Mrs Tennant, to

see them and know that they are responsible. I can see through it, Mrs Tennant, and I know."

I make no response. Do I assume that her calling me Mrs Tennant is deliberate or a mistake of the moment? Are we going to take this away in our own sequestered way, each assuming a greatness over the other that sensitivity and understanding should disallow. I hope not. I will happily concede a special knowing of my son to this woman, happily concede to their love, but I insist on my belonging. I am sacred, comfort me, comfort me with the godless care one human soul can afford another. My name is Louise, mother of Joseph, wife of John, comfort us all. "I don't doubt your knowing, Joanne, not for a moment."

"They are culpable. I have no doubt about that. As far as I am concerned they drove every car that struck him."

I nod my agreement. Of course they are culpable. I know the way blame works in these matters. I hear the sound of it every day. I say: "There is a piece of music goes over and over in my head whenever I think of Joseph lying in the road, a very beautiful piece of music." She nods her head as if she understands, and perhaps she really does.

Chapter Twenty-Two

It is cold in London. I sit in the window and look down into the street. I have my glass of wine but I'm sipping it, taking pleasure from it. After days of bright, brittle sunlight there has been a late cold snap. There is even the promise of late snow. I don't believe it. I have come to believe in the extinction of snow. I also know that I am against it. I want to challenge defeat. I have had enough of it. I am due to return to work soon. I have just rung Vivien to tell her the news. She is delighted of course. She feels responsible. To her mind she has seen me through my period of turmoil, something we will look back on together as lost time. I also rang her as soon as I got back from France, apologizing for letting her down regarding the pamper session, which she immediately dismissed, and since then she has again been ringing regularly. We were both sorry not to have said goodbye when she left London the last time. We neither have tried to explain it. I haven't told her any details about my journey but will, when we meet, two sisters together. Strangely she hasn't asked. I am pleased about that.

My counsellor assumes I've moved on. I would challenge that, except there isn't any point. Time is not linear. I have moved nowhere. Everything stays with me, my sacred world of love. I need love. I need occupation. I have agreed to return after Easter. The facile symbolism of it disappoints me. The world is full of symbolism though, connections, compositions, constructions. It is there in the golden section, in poetry, in nature, inference and possibility. It is in our way of seeing.

I am told that further development of Nivis has been suspended. Joanne keeps in touch. I don't know what our relationship is. We deal with each other with a certain piety. We share something deep and unspoken, without fully articulating what that is. On one level of course it is the memory of my beautiful boy, but there is something else that we neither can fully decipher. I took the material they had been collecting to Paris and put it into the hands of Dominique Dufour. Joanne reasoned that she and Pierre-Yves Moreau were known as activists, though not that they were together. I was a grieving mother asking too many questions. The handover of Joseph's work took place in a small grocery in the village, the only grocery in the village. I still can't quite believe the fear and the looking, wondering about everyone, doubting them all. The handover was terrifying. A young woman bumped into me, apologized profusely and began dusting me down and straightening me, whilst at the same time passing a shopping bag into my hand, the same as the one I was carrying which she took from me. At the time it felt like theft. I can still see glimpses of her small, nervous face. The overall picture is gone, but the detail remains, the nervousness, the need to trust.

Taking leave of Pierre-Yves Moreau was difficult. In no time there had developed so much trust and friendship between us, indeed, what could only be described as a subtle and developing love. He brought Joseph back to me, made us whole again, and for that I will always be grateful. Even in the midst of his grief he knew it was right to care, to care and reclaim. His is such a tired yet tireless

229

spirit. Instead I trusted Bill, trusted and gave myself to him – or whoever. I am to blame for a reckless, mistaken, error of judgement. If only I had met Pierre-Yves Moreau first it all could have been so different.

Of course that is true of everything. We engage with the world we have, not the one that might be. Time and space are arbitrary, subject to luck and experimentation, and we have to be engaged, connected, we have no other choice. I think that is what was in Dominique Dufour's expression as she took the papers from me. I think she saw it as my redemption. I had committed an act. I don't think I would dispute that. My redemption, for want of a better word, was in that and in so much else. I must admit that I felt momentarily uneasy as I handed over the file. But I remembered my gratitude to Dominique Dufour and my need to believe in her. Of course she is honest. Hers is a good mission.

John's father, Jim, is dead. Jim is dead. The home tried to contact me but were unable. They involved the police but with no success. I went to visit when I got back to London. It seemed the right thing to do. A very troubled woman said that they had been trying to contact me. I knew from the tone of her voice what was coming. Apparently his breathing had become difficult. He was bedbound for a number of days. He was quite a fighter she said. He didn't go easily. I don't know whether I was pleased or not that he didn't go easily. It suggests he was waiting for something, or more accurately someone, I suppose.

I rang John to tell him. I told him that his father had died quietly and peacefully. I was sorry that I couldn't have let him know earlier, but I didn't feel any guilt. At the end of the day I was trying to find out the truth about our son. All truths are ours, John's and mine. We are inseparable. Our stories are one. My redemption is in the unflagging, endless love I feel for him and know he feels for me. He said that he was sorry that he had not been there, but believed his father would understand, and then told me he would be home for Easter. He said he was more than ready for it.

My beautiful son is dead and I need occupation. I have things to do, curiosities to investigate. I want my mission to be a good one. That was always the hope.

It is beginning to snow. The weather reports may prove to be right. I have every hope that these large drifting flakes will lie. For a while the whole visible world will be white. There will be no boredom in that at all.